"*Relief Map* is a first-rate literary thriller in the Hitchcock tradition, where a police blockade turns a small town into a pressure cooker, secrets unravel in the heat, and the real danger comes not from the criminals, but from the police and the not-so-innocent bystanders. A quietly chilling novel about the loss of innocence against the backdrop of the modern war on terrorism."

—AMY STEWART, author of *Girl Waits with Gun*

"Moving between the perspective of a teenaged girl and a desperate fugitive, *Relief Map* combines elements of the coming-of-age pastoral with the political thriller. Beautifully written, heartfelt, and mesmerizing, this book puts Rosalie Knecht on the map as a major talent."

—DAN CHAON, author of *Await Your Reply*

RELIEF MAP

ROSALIE KNECHT

 TIN HOUSE BOOKS / Portland, Oregon & Brooklyn, New York

Published by Tin House Books, Portland, Oregon, and Brooklyn, New York

Distributed by W. W. Norton and Company

Library of Congress Cataloging-in-Publication Data

Names: Knecht, Rosalie.
Title: Relief map / by Rosalie Knecht.
Description: First U.S. edition. | Portland, Oregon : Tin House Books, 2016.
Identifiers: LCCN 2015031307 | ISBN 9781941040225 (alk. paper)
Classification: LCC PS3611.N43 R45 2016 | DDC 813/.6--dc23
LC record available at http://lccn.loc.gov/2015031307

First US Edition 2016
Printed in USA
Interior design by Diane Chonette
www.tinhouse.com

For Patricia Fairbanks

1

Livy went outside when the clanging in the valley finally became unbearable. It was a hollow, high-pitched noise, as if someone were striking a bell with a hammer. Livy was babysitting, and the baby was asleep just then by some miracle, and if he woke up because of this idiot noise she thought she might lose her mind. It was too hot, and she did not particularly like the baby: he was thirteen months, just old enough to hit people when he was unhappy.

She stood on the front porch and squinted into the bright morning. The porch was wide and neat, lined with Astroturf. The corner store sat just below the house, and across the road the Church of God in Christ raised its white bell tower against the green and gray mass of the hill. Collier Road, climbing past the front steps of the

house and disappearing in the trees beyond the playground, lay stunned in the August heat. There was no
one out anywhere. The clanging noise began again, and
then slackened and died away. Livy hopped down the
steps and into the road, barefoot, scanning the quiet
houses up and down the valley.

Collier Road was steepest where she stood, and she
could see down into the backyards of the houses along
the loop of the Lomath Creek. They were built anxiously
close to White Horse Road, clinging to the hip of the
hill while the land dropped away to the floodplain behind them. The damp backyards were full of bicycles,
disassembled cars, and half-built projects of various
kinds, some of them clearly aspiring to locomotion: go-
karts, rafts, plywood, and stray wheels. She could see the
glitter of arc welding in Brian Carroll's backyard. She
rose up on her toes and shouted his name.

There was no way he could hear her. She glanced
back over her shoulder at the house, at the floral-printed
bedsheets tacked up in the windows to keep out the heat,
the air conditioners dripping and straining, and decided
she could slip away for two minutes. The baby wasn't
big enough to escape from his crib. She padded down
the curving slope toward Brian's house. He was eighteen,
two years older than she was but only one grade ahead,
and she had once overheard him telling a navy recruiter

during a Career Day presentation that his goal in life was either to become a stock car mechanic or die young. Livy reached the edge of his front yard just as the banging sound started up again.

"Brian!" she called. They were not friends. He, like many other boys she knew, projected a mild disdain for girls. She hesitated at the edge of the road, trying to remember if Brian's parents were the type that exploded with rage if anyone stepped over their property lines, and then resolutely put one foot on the grass. There was no car in the driveway. She pushed past a massive azalea bush and into the backyard, nearly tripping over a kiddie pool half filled with silt and rainwater.

Twin black ovals turned toward her as she came around the corner. She glanced from one boy to the other. They were both wearing welding masks. A gutted motorbike lay on its side in the grass. "Brian?" she said to the shorter boy.

He flipped up his mask. "Yeah?"

"What are you doing?"

He gestured at an amputated gas tank lying in a metal pan at his feet, like a swollen kidney. "Working."

"Could you do it later? I'm babysitting Mallory's kid and he's asleep." She folded her arms.

"It's the middle of the day," Brian said. "People can do what they want."

"The power just went out anyway," said the bigger boy, lifting his mask. It was Brian's cousin Dominic Spellar, who lived two doors down. He nudged the extension cord in the grass with one foot.

Brian looked deflated. "I guess you win," he said, pulling the mask off.

"Thank you," Livy said, although they hadn't done anything for her. She turned and disappeared around the side of the house.

The baby was wailing when she got back, and she whispered a few curses into the close, dusty air of the curtained living room. The television and the air conditioner had been murmuring when she stepped outside, but they were both silent now, and the room was stifling already. She climbed the stairs and rescued the baby from his crib. He was red and sweaty, showing his few teeth in outrage, and she tried shushing and patting him as she came back down the stairs. Babysitting was all right, but there were easier ways to make money. She had another job waiting tables at the restaurant in the Lomath Sportsmen's Club, the shooting range complex that sat at the junction of the Black Rock and Lomath Creeks. She preferred waitressing to babysitting, because it paid more and she didn't feel bad taking her money at the end of the day. Mallory, the baby's mother, always wrote her a check and then asked her to wait to cash it, and then spent too much time apologizing.

Livy carried the baby out to the porch, and to her relief he quieted in the breeze coming down the hill. She persuaded him to nap in his car seat on the porch swing and sat beside him, pushing off gently with her feet, reading a book on dream interpretation she'd found in the bathroom.

The baby's mother came home at two and was surprised by the blackout. She worked at a hotel half an hour away and there'd been no problem there. She said it was typical, hinting at neglect. Lomath was the kind of place where problems like this appeared to fit into a grand pattern of municipal slights. Potholes multiplied in the roads; telephone poles tipped over in heavy rain and were left dangling for hours before utility trucks came.

Livy walked home, and then couldn't think what to do with the rest of her day. The quiet of her house, denuded of its electrical buzzing, made her restless. She was making a pot of coffee on the stove when her friend Nelson knocked perfunctorily on the door and edged into the kitchen.

"Are you working today?" Livy said. "I was thinking of going to St. Stanis."

Nelson poured himself a cup of coffee. He was tall and thin, half Irish and half Filipino, and had a faintly

evasive manner with most people, although not with
Livy. "Maybe. I thought you were going to be at the restaurant today."

"No, I switched with the Saturday girl."

"It always smells like shit at St. Stanis," Nelson re-
marked.

"It's just the sulfur," Livy said. "It'll be nice. I'm sick
of being hot."

It was easy to persuade him. They borrowed his sister's
car for the short drive to St. Stanis, which was a quarry
and a broad, noisy creek out in more open country. A few
concession stands and T-shirt shops painted in ice-cream
colors clustered along the road above the creek. They
parked in a gravel lot and walked down the trail, waving
away gnats and conjecturing about poison oak.

"Is this it?"

"No, too many leaves, I think."

"Is this it, then?"

The creek was full of swimmers and sunbathers, and
Livy felt a kind of benevolence in the air: old people and
babies in swimsuits, a lack of vanity that suggested they
were all off the hook for the afternoon. Livy was sixteen and still trying to get used to herself. She had dark
hair that failed to distinguish itself, and skin that did not
seem to conceal her blood and bones as thoroughly as
other people's did. She was growing uncomfortably fast,

so fast that stretch marks had appeared on her knees and lower back, like invisible ink revealed by a fire. She feared this growth would continue indefinitely. As the weather got warmer she'd outgrown her clothes and taken to wearing boys' T-shirts, the kind that came in packs of three.

Nelson set his glasses on a rock and pulled his shirt off quickly, one hand at the back of his collar, without any show of self-consciousness. He could be casual and fluid, sure that no one was paying any attention to him. Livy envied him for it. He dropped into the water. "*Cold*," he said, as if reprimanding it. Livy floated, looking up at the tall, flat-bottomed clouds. There was a low chatter all around them of water running and people talking in their encampments on the rocks. A couple of girls nearby began to giggle and Livy looked up at them sharply. They might have been looking in Nelson's direction; the sun was in her eyes and she couldn't tell. She felt proprietary about Nelson. She didn't like to have other people peer into the comfortable space they shared. The sexual interest of other girls was like a dye in the water, blooming and spreading, coloring everything.

She glanced at him to see if he'd noticed. He was brown-skinned now after two months of summer, long-armed. He had just cut his hair as short as he could; the limit was defined by his mother, who controlled his clipper settings. Mrs. Tela loved his hair, mourned its loss, waited anxiously for its return. It was thick and dark and stiff, and it curled if he let it get long enough.

"I was supposed to get a call about that job today," he said, frowning. He had applied for a job at a sporting goods store in Beckford, which paid two dollars more per hour than his current job, serving gelato from bins covered with gold foil at the Hareford Plaza Court. He disliked the job because the customers were constantly disappointed by the small portions: four dollars for a dollop of raspberry in a paper cup, with a tiny short-handled spoon jutting pretentiously from the top. All day long he handed the little cups to people and watched their faces fall. "I put my house phone number on the application," he said. "I should have put my cell."

"Your house phone's not working?" Livy said.

"No. Is yours?"

"I don't know, I haven't tried to call anybody." Water burbled in her ears. She pushed her toes into the sand. "Don't the phones usually still work when the power's out?" She was trying to remember a cartoon about tornadoes that she'd seen on public TV as a kid. Weren't there separate circuits, one for the phones and one for the power, coiling and backtracking through a cartoon town?

"I guess so," he said.

"Do you ever wish you still lived in the city?" she said. Nelson had moved from Philadelphia with his parents and sister when he was thirteen, into a blue house high up on Collier Road, past the playground, in a little niche that had been carved into the hill by earthmovers.

"Why? Because they have working utilities?" he said.

"For one thing."

He laughed. "Sometimes, I guess." He looked up into the overhanging trees. "If you're a kid it's not that much fun." On his arrival in Lomath, he had flattered her with his ignorance of plants. She was the one who had shown him how to salve a nettle sting with jewelweed.

"Horsefly," he said.

She was watching a couple of boys mock-wrestling, showing off in the water for the two girls on the boulder. They were yelling and splashing, darkening the rocks.

"Horsefly," Nelson said again, but she was slow turning and he was there already, brushing it off her shoulder. When the horseflies came you had to dive. She dove.

✳

Revaz twisted his ankle on a stone in the train station. He was shocked by how much it hurt. It was a bit of gravel from between the railroad ties, kicked up onto the platform where he was the only passenger to disembark, and in the dark he stepped on it in his soft-bottomed tennis shoes—they were nearly worn through at the ball of the foot and offered very little support—and his ankle rolled. The twinge followed him as he limped down the steps and made a cautious turn onto a side street where a row of asphalt-shingled houses faced a rising bank of weeds.

He was unsettled by the quiet of the street. It was only eleven o'clock at night, but no cars passed as he skirted the edge of the town, and he saw few lights in the windows. He stopped in the glare of a gas station to consult his map, and then headed right, under the high arches of a bridge. It was only a mile to the cluster of houses marked *Lomath* on the map.

He was tired. He had been too nervous to eat on the train. He hadn't eaten since breakfast, which had been at five o'clock that morning, in a diner in Philadelphia that had exhaled a puff of hot oil when he'd opened the door. He'd had to order by pointing at a plate of eggs and potatoes and sausages being eaten by a man at the next table. He regretted how little English he could remember from his secondary school days. The alphabet had slipped away from him. Some words looked a little familiar, and he could say *please* and *thank you* and *go*, and also *I*, but otherwise he was helpless. Remembering the food now sharpened his hunger. He pushed his mind out, away from his stomach, into the night air.

It had been only four days since he was at home in his own country, in his own apartment. His own balcony, from which a narrow strip of the green river was visible when the leaves were off the lime trees in the winter. He would probably never see that apartment or that street again. His pulse had not slowed to normal since Wednesday, he thought, and it was Sunday now. He had tried to sleep in the airport and on both turbulent flights but had startled awake over and over, choking for breath, flailing with his right arm, his good arm, upsetting the old woman in the seat next to him. He was too aware of his heart now. His hands went to it whenever he needed to think. He had taken a month's worth of his blood pressure pills with him and he kept checking for the orange bottle in the outer pocket of the old backpack he had brought.

Lomath announced itself with a green metal sign. Revaz climbed off the road just after the bend and found a dry spot in the lee of a rotting sofa that had been dumped over the guardrail. The ground dropped away steeply below him, but he could see nothing in the darkness. There was an ounce or two of whiskey left in the little bottle he'd bought in Philadelphia; he drank it and fell asleep.

It was a damp night. He woke just as the sky was beginning to lighten and found a trio of slugs on the laces of his tennis shoes. At the bottom of the slope there was a creek that he had only heard in the darkness the night before. He could see the white glint of it now, its busy flow around stands of trees. He pictured himself perched there beside the decaying hulk of the sofa, his thin hair wild, in undignified shoes. A curtain of despair threatened to drop again, but he pushed it away.

Revaz got up stiffly and walked toward the first houses of Lomath, staying back in the woods. He was afraid of dogs more than anything. He could skirt the village easily—it was rarely more than one house and one road deep, and the hills ringed it protectively. He walked and walked along the hills, keeping the houses to his left. His ankle was better than it had been the night before; it wasn't sprained, then. As the sun was rising he found himself at the top of the ridge on the east side of Lomath, his heart a little lightened by the gold in the air. He sat on a stone and watched the valley below him flood with light. There was a small white house with a vegetable garden far below, tucked into a bend in the creek.

The power went out in Lomath while he slept the day away in a rank-smelling deer blind in a tree just over the top of the ridge. Flies harried him while he slept.

※

The power was still out at seven thirty the next morning when Livy's father woke her. She had a dental checkup at nine, and since Greg Marko was re-shingling a house not far from the dental center that day, he planned to drop her off on his way to work. She took too long getting dressed, out of practice in the summer at getting up early, and he had to come back twice and knock on her door. She brushed her teeth with extra care.

They pulled out of the driveway just after eight thirty and drove down Prospect to White Horse Road. When they came around the turn they saw a van and a truck stopped haphazardly in the road, lights flashing.

"Accident?" Livy said.

Her father downshifted steadily, not yet committing to the brakes. "No, those are all police," he said. Livy hoisted herself up and peered out through the truck's windshield. He was right; they were marked with the Maronne Police Department logo. Maronne was a steel town a mile away, and Lomath was a small unincorporated outlier of it. An officer got out of the van and walked toward them slowly, holding up one hand.

Livy's father put the truck in neutral. A couple of sawhorses were set up across the road with chains looped between them. Livy was alert now, her hands spread flat on her lap. Her father had made a long speech to her about the police as soon as she got her license, with heavy stress on politeness, keeping your hands where they could see them, and describing any movement you were about to make before you made it. He illustrated his points with many anecdotes about traffic stops in his youth, when the cops always said something about his hair, which was long then. They would insinuate that he had drugs, and that if he didn't have them now he would have them soon, and that he was likely to get stopped again, in any event.

Livy had never been in a traffic stop before. She watched the approaching policeman with interest.

"See some ID?" the cop said.

Livy's father nodded. "Let me get out my wallet," he said. He produced his driver's license, and the officer examined it for a minute and then peered into his face and handed it back.

"We're looking for somebody," the officer said. He opened a plastic folder with a friendly, lazy flourish. Inside was a blurry color photo of a middle-aged man. Livy leaned over from her seat to see, but her father gave her a look and she settled back. "Have you seen this person?" said the officer.

Her father shrugged. "No, I don't think so."

"You're sure? Maybe he looks different, maybe he hasn't been shaving?"

Her father leaned closer. "No. Sorry." He looked up at the cop. "Is he here?"

"We've been asked to close the roads. And I would ask you to return to your home, sir."

"Is he dangerous?" His voice rose a little.

"I couldn't say, sir," said the policeman. "This is coming down from a higher level. Like I said, I'm going to have to ask you to return to your home."

Livy's father put the truck in reverse and executed a tentative three-point turn in the too-narrow road. As soon as they had moved out of range of the policeman, Livy cleared her throat, scanning the undergrowth on the side of the road for signs of impending action. "Do you think somebody broke out of Emeryville?" she said.

"Could be, I guess. Seems like a lot of trouble to go to for a minimum-security breakout, though."

"Is it normal? They just block everything off?"

"If they're looking for somebody, I guess they could."

They tried the other routes out of the valley. At the next one they found another roadblock, another car, and another polite cop. He asked for her father's identification and showed him the photo, even after he said he'd seen it already. The officer walked in a circle around the truck and lifted the tarp in the back, frowning seriously at the bundles of cedar shakes underneath. Livy and her father did not speak to each other as they turned slowly around and drove away. Her father had turned the radio off, as he sometimes did when he was about to merge around construction or attempt an especially difficult highway on-ramp. Livy was flexing and relaxing her hands in turn, one after the other, like a cat. It was now only ten minutes until her appointment time, which was not long enough to get there, and if she was late she would have to spend at least an extra hour sitting in the waiting room and listening to the faint squeal of drills through the walls before another time slot opened up. She was afraid of the dentist, and her teeth already ached from clenching her jaw. There was one last route out of the valley, which was Somersburg Road, but as they came around the curve they saw that the intersection was blocked, this time with a low plastic barricade and a strip of tire-puncturing stainless steel. "Shit," Livy said, and was not rebuked for it. Her father gamely put the truck in neutral again.

The roadblock was manned by a lone officer chewing gum in a cruiser. He made no move to get out of his car. Livy glanced back and forth between her father and the policeman, the two men regarding each other through their windshields. After a long pause, her father opened his door and stepped down from the truck. He ambled toward the car, studiously casual. The two men began to talk in a way that looked friendly. After a moment, not wanting to miss anything, Livy got out of the truck herself.

"He's from the Balkans," the cop was saying.

"Really?" her father said.

"That's what they told us. These federal guys, you know." The cop rolled his eyes. He was older, gray-haired, red-faced. He seemed generous with information, gesturing loosely with the hand that dangled over the sill of his car door.

"Why would he be here?" her father said, waving his hand illustratively at the guardrail, the row of trash cans at the end of a driveway, the ragged pasture across the road.

The cop rolled his eyes again. "FBI guys show up yesterday with a bunch of trucks and now they're in charge. Who knows."

"Is that why the power's out?" her father said.

"That I don't know. That would be the utility company. You should call."

"The phones are out too."

"Really? That's probably the feds, then."

✳

They were back at the house by nine. They sat in the truck in the yard for a little while before going in, searching for the local stations on the radio, but couldn't find them: it was always hard to get a signal on the weaker frequencies down in the valley. After a few minutes her father turned the radio off, muttering about running down the battery. Livy trailed after him into the house. His step was quicker than normal, and he kept putting his hands in his pockets and taking them out again.

In the kitchen he turned on the front burner but it failed to light for several seconds, and he had to stop to wave the gas away. "How about pancakes?" he said to Livy.

"Sure," she said. She hovered around the edges of the kitchen, waiting for a clearer response from him, but there was none. She felt lucky not to be at the dentist; beyond that the morning felt distant and abstract. Her father made pancakes and she took all the toppings she could think of out of the cabinet and lined them up on the table, first in a straight row, then in a circle with a jar of blueberry jam at the center. Her father tended to retreat into an implausible calm when anything frightening or strange happened. She remembered once, when she was seven, watching from the living room window while he walked at a stately pace from the far edge of the yard, shirtless despite the coolness of an early spring day, revealing when he arrived in the kitchen that his shirt was wrapped tightly around his mangled and bleeding right hand. He had been using a rope thrown over the branch of a sugar maple to hoist the engine out of an ancient Volvo, and his right hand had gotten pinned in the engine compartment and twisted, almost severing his index finger. When she offered to dial 911 for him as she had learned in school—white, shaking, saucer-eyed at the blood soaking through the checked fabric—he had said, "No, I'll drive. Do you know how to heat up a cup of coffee?" Livy had successfully heated the coffee, though she was not normally allowed to use the stove. She had also operated the gearshift all the way to the hospital. Her father was left with a thick scar down the length of the finger and limited range of motion to the second knuckle. Livy had asked him years later about the coffee, and why he wasn't worried that the delay might cost him his finger, but he claimed not to remember it.

Her father started the pancake batter and then borrowed Livy's cell phone, although its service was terrible in the valley—Livy usually walked to the top of their long driveway if she wanted to use it—and called the owner of the roof he was supposed to be working on in Hareford. Livy heard him explaining what was happening, apologizing for the delay in the job, and then what sounded like several rounds of mutual complaint over the way things were run in the world today. The police roadblocks were folded into an everyday rant about traffic.

Livy's mother, Mariel, came into the kitchen in an old bathrobe toward the end of the conversation and stood in her husband's periphery with a questioning look until he got off the phone. She was a charge nurse on the evening shift at the hospital in Maronne, and she rarely found her husband in the house when she woke up in the morning. During the week, their days cross-stitched past each other, and Livy was not used to being in the house with both of them at once except on the weekends. She found herself absent-mindedly digging the cloth napkins out of a drawer to use with breakfast, as if it were a holiday.

Her father explained what had happened while he made a second pot of coffee. Her mother listened and frowned. At first she looked irritated, but as he spoke her face softened into blankness. When he was done she sat for a minute, her hand on her forehead. "Oh, Greg," she said.

Livy looked impatiently at them. Why were they both being so quiet, so slow-moving about this? She wanted energetic theorizing to match the weirdness of the occasion. But for a few seconds the Markos merely looked at each other, wide-eyed.

"So he's hiding here?" Livy said, prodding.

"I doubt it," her mother said. "Why would anybody come here? I mean, from halfway around the world?"

"It didn't sound like they really knew what was going on," her father said, turning his back now to watch the bubbles rising in the pancakes. "The FBI's calling the shots."

"And the Maronne PD is screwing it up," her mother said with sudden conviction. She bundled her robe up with one hand and pushed her hair out of her face with the other. "They don't know what the hell they're doing. Remember when they were after that kid for armed robbery in Maronne? He hid in his mother's basement in the west end for three weeks. It took them *three weeks* to get around to checking his mother's basement."

Livy was running a spoon back and forth across the surface of the table, a habit that she couldn't break and that annoyed her mother. "How long do you think we're going to be stuck in here?" she said.

"Who knows," her mother said. "I guess they can do whatever they want, can't they?"

Her father cleared his throat. "Let's not get panicky."

"I'm not getting panicky," her mother said. "I just hope they're out of the way before I have to go to work."

"What do you think he did?" Livy said. "It must be something big."

"Who knows," her father said.

"But what do you think?"

"I don't *know*, Livy."

His tone stopped her. She busied herself setting the table.

❊

Livy went up the hill to find Nelson, wanting to compare notes. There were a few people sitting outside the corner store, including Jocelyn, the owner, who was smoking a cigarette at the bottom of the steps and waving her arms. These emphatic gestures looked strange on her; she was normally so quiet, so slump-shouldered, a thin woman hunched in on herself. Livy went by on the other side of the road, out of earshot.

Nelson's house, sitting up on the hillside, always seemed to be further along in the day than her own. She was out of breath when she reached the front door: the yard was an absurd, ankle-twisting slope. Nelson opened the door with a half bottle of orange soda in one hand and a cell phone in the other. "The battery's dying," he said. "But my dad wants me to keep it on in case the FBI wants to call and apologize for the inconvenience."

His parents and sister were sitting at the kitchen table. "It's in case your *lola* calls," Nelson's father said, using the Tagalog word for grandmother. Nelson's Filipino grandparents lived in the suburbs on the New Jersey side of Philadelphia. "Don't be a smartass. I left her a message, she's going to be worried."

"Do you know about the roads?" Nelson's mother said to Livy.

"Yeah. They said he's from the Balkans." The geographical phrase was already starting to warp on her tongue, becoming more than it was. It didn't mean anything to her, really.

"He is? I didn't hear that," Mrs. Tela said.

"I doubt that," said Mr. Tela. "When the cops are here it's always about the goddamn drug addicts down at the store, that kid Jeremiah and his drug dealer friends. You see them out on the bridge, don't you? I drive through at ten, eleven o'clock at night and they're standing in the middle of the road like *I* have no right to be there." He expanded and slackened as he said this, like an uncoiling spring. "Ought to throw them out. And Jocelyn too. Get that whole family out of here."

Livy could think of nothing to say to that, since he seemed to be indulging in a private fantasy in which he lived in a neighborhood where difficult people could be forced to leave—someplace like where her friend Elena lived, where clotheslines were prohibited and flags had to be approved by a board and you could be fined for painting your garage a different color from your house. She glanced at Nelson, who had adopted the blank expression he favored with his parents.

Mrs. Tela tapped her fingers on the table. Her eyes were red. She was a nervous woman. "How long is it going to be, anyway?" she said. She didn't seem to expect an answer. Livy shrugged and made an apologetic face. Nelson moved off down the hall toward his bedroom and Livy turned to follow him, relieved.

"Keep the door open," Mrs. Tela called after them. Neither Livy nor Nelson reacted to this in any visible way. Livy hated Mrs. Tela. She particularly hated her every time she reiterated this unnecessary rule, which Livy believed was meant to humiliate her, to make it hard for her to look Nelson in the eye.

Livy had always thought of herself as a plain girl, at best inoffensive to look at. In elementary school she'd been mocked for her clothes, mostly secondhand items she chose with a sensibility shaped by *Anne of Green Gables* as much as anything else—pinafores and homemade sweaters, interspersed with corduroy pants on gym days. The meanest kids were a group of boys who made it clear to her that while her clothes were bad, her face was the real problem: her teeth stuck out, and her cheeks were too round, and her nose was shaped wrong. She also said stupid things, and once made the serious mistake of trying to argue value with a boy who was chanting "Goodwill shoes! Goodwill shoes! Goodwill shoes!" at her with such excitement that he was spraying her with spit. She knew she no longer looked as awkward as she had when she was nine and ten, but she was still mostly afraid of boys, afraid of the careless and vicious way they could judge the girls around them. For most of the time they had been friends she was relieved to find that Nelson didn't seem to think of her as a girl at all, but as a person who liked and disliked the same things he did, and with the same energy.

Nelson's room was small and bright, facing down the hill. The walls were white. His sister had painted her room a shade of blue-green called "Twilight Meadow" the summer before, but Nelson's room had stayed white. He didn't seem to understand why anyone would go to any effort to change the appearance of a wall.

When the door was shut Livy said, "Jesus Christ." Someone was mowing a lawn, somewhere up the hill.

"He's been talking about drugs this whole time," Nelson said. "It's like he had a speech prepared." Livy saw his eyes go reflexively toward the desk drawer where he kept his pot in a little tin box.

"Your computer looks so dead," Livy said. She wasn't used to seeing the monitor dark, hulking in the corner by the window. He made music on it, inscrutable songs that were full of crinkly explosions and bookended by minutes and minutes of peppy dance beats. Livy had listened to several songs with him recently and was reminded of electric fencing. They had been stoned at the time, so she told him this, which seemed to satisfy him. She was the only one who had heard the songs. He was a private person. "This is crazy," she added. She was aware that she was enjoying it a little, the way she enjoyed thunderstorms.

"My mom thought it was because of Maurice and Bev," Nelson said. "They had another fight last night." Maurice Carden and his girlfriend lived in one of the twin houses by the bridge. Sometimes, to punctuate their fights, Maurice would appear in the yard and fire a small-bore rifle into the air. Then he would stand there for a while, as if waiting for the bullet to come down.

Livy did a lap of the room, looking things over. The Tela house made her restless. "Do you want to go see the roadblock?" she said.

He raised his eyebrows. "Okay, let me get my shoes."

They slipped out the front door without being questioned. It was a steep walk up to the roadblock, and by the time it was in view they were both sweating and slightly out of breath. They saw the police truck from a distance and walked toward it as confidently as they could, heads up, hands out of their pockets. The policeman stayed in the truck. When they got close they saw that he was leaning back in his seat, one arm trailing out the window. He watched them with some interest. They stopped a few feet from the yellow sawhorse and looked at him for a long moment.

"Get back, kids," he said.

Livy took a half step back and ran into Nelson; she hadn't realized he'd come up so close. "Can we get by?" she said. She smiled. In the last few years she had developed, somewhat against her own will, a lilting way of asking questions that stripped them of aggression. Nelson hovered behind her, suddenly tense and quiet, and Livy could see that the cop's eyes drifted toward him even as he spoke to her.

"No," the officer said.

"Why not?" She smiled again.

The cop sat up, stretched his arms, and sighed. "You want to obstruct an investigation?" he said. "You want to get arrested? Get back."

On the other side of the sawhorse, a chain was stretched across the road. Yellow plastic ribbons hung from it, perfectly still. The policeman smiled. He waggled his fingers at them.

They got back. They stopped to think in the shade of the store at the bottom of the hill. Livy had an unsettled feeling in her stomach, as if she had briefly been hung upside down.

"That guy was a dick," Nelson said. "Let's go to the other one. The one at Somersburg Road. We could walk up the creek." He straightened up as he said this, animated by a rush of righteousness. Livy was beginning to feel nervous. "Maybe we should give it a rest," she said.

Nelson frowned at his shoes, and then frowned at the horizon. "That guy was a dick," he said again.

"Yeah." She watched him. He was squinting through his glasses. If she were alone, she would have dropped the project then, but she pushed things further when he was around, not wanting to disabuse him of his apparent belief that she was daring and adventurous. She doubted that anyone else thought this about her; their school was strictly divided between good kids and bad kids. So she tended to go with him on his mild delinquencies—cutting class, walking into Maronne late at night to smoke a spliff by the sodium-lit scrapyard. This was a particular favorite, the two of them sitting quietly against the fence by the piles of wrecked cars and gutted appliances. It was dramatic and filthy and quiet. Livy was prone to apocalyptic, self-aggrandizing thoughts there, and she suspected that Nelson was too. A security guard had shined a flashlight in their faces once but Livy had apologized so elaborately that he waved them away. Adults reacted differently to boys and girls at that age, and they seemed to go easier on Nelson when she was with him.

"Let me get an iced tea first," she said.

They stopped in the store and bought one from Jocelyn, who was staring moodily into a freezer full of melted Popsicles, and then they walked north, slapping mosquitoes. Before the road left the cover of the trees they slipped down the bank to the stream. It was shallow there, with sandbars along the far side that they could walk on easily and quietly. A margin of trees protected them from the lower pasture of an underused dairy farm that belonged to a lean artistic couple named Insky. The farmhouse stood at the top of the hill, gamely ignoring a highway that roared behind it. Livy had lived her whole life at the bottom of the valley, and the high yellow sweep of cleared land had always been her horizon. When she was about nine Livy started a game of crossing the creek in secret and running through the Inskys' lower pastures, pulling watercress out of their spring, walking bent-legged on the cow paths through their waste of brambles, applying names to things and annexing territories to herself. The Inskys never seemed to notice. They were friends of her parents', and they were unusual in that group for having no children. This made them seem somehow more grown-up than the other grown-ups. They sometimes invited Livy's parents over for dinner, and Livy was not asked to come along. Her parents would pick their way across the creek in the early evening, one of them holding a wine bottle by the neck, and come home after ten in an exuberant, chatty mood. It wasn't that the Inskys disliked children, exactly; they were never hostile to those in their path. They just projected a lack of interest in accommodating them. This added to the thrill Livy found in roaming through the fringes of their farm during the period of her childhood when she spent most of her time outdoors. She always thought she might catch them in some shocking act, the contours of which were vague in her mind.

Livy still felt a faint sense of ownership when she was near the Insky farm, and this gave her confidence. She led the way as they waded toward the blockade, chatting about the defects of people they knew in school. At a narrow bend in the creek she stepped sideways on a stone, bruised her foot, and almost dropped her shoes. She cursed and wobbled, noisily regaining her balance.

"Shh," Nelson said. He pointed up at the road, where they could just see a police cruiser through a gap in the bushes, the edge of the Maronne city seal visible on the driver's side door: a mill building hidden coyly behind a foregrounded tree.

Livy quieted, clutching at an overhanging willow for balance. "God, it's so close," she whispered. She could see the scratches in the paint around the door handle. Another vehicle was approaching from the Lomath side, a truck by the sound of it, invisibly rolling to a stop at the barricade. The driver's side door of the police cruiser opened, and Livy and Nelson ducked in unison, putting their hands in the water to catch their balance, as the police officer stepped out of the car and walked out of their narrow line of sight. Their view of the truck that had approached was blocked by a row of multiflora rosebushes in full bloom, but the voices came down to them clearly over the burbling of the creek. She searched out Nelson's eyes. She was hardly breathing.

"See your ID?" said the policeman on the road.

She could hear feet shifting on the gravel, and then Ron Cash's voice. He lived in one of the houses up on the hill, a tall white man with a perpetually sunburned bald head and a leg that wouldn't bend at the knee. He was a difficult neighbor, a sore spot. He had a three-wheeler that he rode back and forth on the low road on summer afternoons, the noise of the engine like a zipper splitting open the peaceful air. He hunted deer out of season, blocked the Greens in when he parked, and responded to all criticism with threats. He was a playground aide at the elementary school, a difficult job for someone whose disability was so easy for children to imitate, and Livy still carried a grudge over something he'd done when she was one of the children under his supervision. She'd been out at the farthest ragged edge of the playing fields at Maronne Elementary with a friend named Kim, a small girl with an insane laugh and constantly dirty nails who was her classmate for only that one year. They liked that spot because of the tall grass. Livy had invented a game that she called Prairie Fire, in which they would go right up to the edge of the mowed lawn and stare into the bluestem and Indian grass and Livy would narrate the progress of an imaginary conflagration roaring toward them from the YMCA at the top of the hill. "Here it comes," she would say. "Look, there goes that little tree, and the other one next to it, poof! And now it's going faster because of the wind, it jumped over the road!" It was a game of nerves: they would stand and face the wall of fire hand in hand until her description of it reached the very edge of the grass, an arm's length from where they stood, and then they would break hands and run as fast as they could toward the low red-painted school building behind them. The first to touch the wall was the survivor; the unfortunate laggard was burned to death in the fire. Livy always won the game because the fire was hers and she had longer legs, but despite this unfairness Kim loved to play, collapsing against the school wall in a hysterical heap each time, not caring that the ground was muddy there from water dripping over the eaves, chirping "Burnt! Burnt!" when she could catch her breath. Once Livy had looked up from her spot by the wall, still laughing, and Ron Cash was standing there in his school-issued blue windbreaker.

"You girls were holding hands," he said. "Knock that off."

It had ruined the game. They were eight or nine, just old enough to understand his insinuation, and they avoided each other for several days afterward.

Ron Cash's voice was high and prone to cracking, and she had always associated this with his knee: a stiffness in both cases, perhaps caused by the same formative accident. She strained to hear him over the rustling of leaves. "I can't get by?" he said.

She was no longer looking at Nelson, but down at her hands instead, the better to concentrate on keeping still and quiet. She did not want to get caught there, though she supposed they weren't breaking any rules, technically speaking. It would be humiliating, that was all. She wished suddenly that she were not overhearing this conversation.

"I can't get through?" said the high, strained voice again. "You're saying I can't?"

"Nobody can get through now," the policeman said.

"You can't block me in like this."

"It's not up to me," said the policeman. "But if you want a problem, you'll get a problem."

"I have places to go."

"Get back in your vehicle, sir. Go on."

Livy was holding on to Nelson's knee, cradling her shoes in her other hand. They looked at each other. Nelson leaned close to her ear and whispered—the barest movement of air—"What is wrong with him?"

"He's an idiot," Livy whispered. They heard the door slam, and then the truck turned laboriously around and headed away down Prospect Road. They sighted the policeman briefly through the gap in the bushes as he got back into his car.

"Let's get out of here," Livy whispered, and Nelson nodded. It was dangerous to overhear humiliation like that. Quavering, wheedling, angry Ron. As soon as they were safely around the bend, they climbed up into the Inskys' pasture and put their shoes on, straightening their stiff backs, relieved to speak in normal tones again.

By eleven thirty, Livy and Nelson were at the store again, having found nothing to satisfy their restlessness at either of their houses, or at the restaurant, or anywhere on the roads. Lomath was half a mile long, anchored at each end by an eighteenth-century textile mill, one of which was now the shooting range and restaurant where Livy worked, the other a large and useless tax burden on a group of carpenters who had bought it collectively decades before in the hope of turning it into apartments. For as long as Livy could remember, the carpenters' mill had contained only two apartments, and the rest of its vast open floor plan was filled with a boggling array of objects placed in storage by anyone willing to pay fifty dollars a year for the privilege: a phalanx of Chevy fenders propped together on the third floor, a mass of bicycle parts on the second, card tables and folding chairs and canoes, boxes and boxes of old *National Lampoons* and *Playboys* cached among winter coats and luggage and rusting tools. The original water-wheel had been amputated from its place over the Black Rock Creek and now lay abandoned in the basement, jutting out from an earthen pit otherwise filled with the engine block of a 1974 Pinto station wagon. Livy had been warned to stay out of the mill on the grounds that she could get tetanus from the rusty door hinges or hantavirus from the piles of mouse shit in the attic, but she sometimes slipped in through one of the ground-floor windows in the back anyway. She liked to leaf through the old magazines and study the dirty cartoons, the plump Playboy bunnies and tailcoated men and the dowager women who kept them apart, a small cast of characters forever stumbling over each other in elevators and darkened rooms. The bunnies were drawn with pink areolae that startled her every time, even after years of returning to the dusty magazines that she vaguely sensed were corny in a way. Maybe it was because the areolae implied that other cartoon characters, elsewhere, were also naked under their clothes. She had shown the cartoons to Nelson when they were thirteen and had seen the same subtle shift happening behind his eyes, before they both turned to mocking the drawings. They leafed quickly past the actual photos, pretending indifference. At twelve, shortly after seeing the magazines for the first time herself, Livy had secretly written five pages of a play in which women in bathing suits kept losing their tops while being chased around a swimming pool by men in tuxedos. She became ashamed of the pages as soon as she'd written them, hid them under her mattress, and burned them in the yard with a box of kitchen matches after her parents had gone to bed.

She and Nelson were, as far as she knew, the only people who trespassed in that mill. The other one had been expanded and converted into a button factory in the 1930s, then was shut down in the 1970s, and had been fertile ground for teenage delinquency during the many years of emptiness that preceded the restaurant and shooting range that occupied it now.

Idling around a mill building, open or closed, operating or hastily abandoned, had been the mainstay of shiftless teenagers in Lomath throughout the entire 250 years that the neighborhood had existed. Lomath had only been built in the first place to house the laborers at the two mills. They were Irishmen and Haitians baited there by recruiters at distant shipyards, and they came and went as the price of cotton rose and fell. Because of their transience it was a settlement of renters, resented and neglected by landlords, and the houses were put up small and square, fast and cheap.

The Marko house was a millworker house, built simply but too solid to fall down, and beside their driveway there were traces of two other, similar houses that had succumbed to fire fifty or a hundred years before. Livy's mother had planted flower beds around the foundations, and she still regularly found bits of charred wood when she turned the earth. Clarence Green claimed that when his own father was young, one of the houses had been occupied by a couple who murdered their child. Livy's parents dismissed this as a lurid rumor, but Livy was inclined to believe it. Lomath was unincorporated, unidentified on most road maps, hidden from the highway and from larger Maronne by its ring of high ridges; she imagined that people there had always felt that no one was watching them.

At the store, Livy and Nelson found Livy's parents talking to Jocelyn, meeting her dark theorizing with polite expressions. The two teenagers nodded hello and went outside to the steps, where other neighbors were chatting and arguing. Clarence and Aurelia Green appeared. "The wires don't go through up there, not by the bypass," Clarence was saying. He was about fifty, black, with short gray hair and a gentle set to his shoulders, and since he worked for the electric company his opinion on the power outage was valuable. "It has to be something they're doing with the whole grid."

"But why are the cops here at the same time?" said Lena Spellar. Her lashless blue eyes looked pinker than usual around the edges. Lena was a hospice nurse, and she sometimes attended continuing-education seminars with Livy's mother, Mariel, who always spoke of the hospice specialization with particular respect. Livy's mother was an intensive care nurse at the hospital, and she said that seeing a patient recover was the single redeeming satisfaction of the profession and she was in awe of any nurse who would willingly forgo it. Livy had always felt hushed around Lena for this reason. She was unobtrusive in public, a chlorinated blonde who spoke little. Dominic, the bigger of the two arc welders, was her son. He was in Livy's grade, and Livy sometimes found herself thinking of him the same way as his mother, so that his sullen, self-contained progress down the halls at school carried the dignity and mystery of close contact with the dying.

"Maybe it's a coincidence," said Clarence. "It could still be a coincidence."

"It's ridiculous," said Paula Carden, a cousin of Clarence's, a foster mother by profession. She kept pausing to push her hair back off her forehead; in the heat, her curls slipped loose from the teeth of her headband, which made her look girlish. "I'm trying to cook all the meat in my freezer before it goes bad."

"Jumping the gun, don't you think?" Clarence said.

"No sense waiting."

"It's always the end of the world with you," Clarence said, rolling his eyes.

By noon a dozen or so neighbors were gathered in front of the store, passing their few pieces of information back and forth. It was clear by then that no cars would be passing, so the adults stood in the middle of the intersection and let their children run around as they pleased.

"It feels like a snow day," Nelson said.

"How do you mean?" Livy said.

"Just kind of exceptional. Everybody stopping what they're supposed to be doing." He nodded toward Dominic Spellar, who was leaning against the wall of the store with Brian Carroll. They had changed out of their welding clothes; Brian was wearing a basketball jersey that was too big for him. "Look, Dominic doesn't look worried."

Livy laughed. "Looks like he's putting all his energy into it, too." Dominic was enormous, broad-shouldered for a high school student and well over six feet tall, and he pressed this advantage constantly with a low, mumbling voice and a way of standing over people that made them worry they might trip over his feet.

"And Brian is feeding off his aura," Livy added. Brian was shoring up his nonchalance with a cigarette, propped against the wall with his bony elbows out. He was the less intimidating of the two cousins, but also less predictable, faster-moving.

A few other teenagers were also pretending to be casual, but the adults were frank about their agitation, clumped together and talking loudly. The talk among them was repetitive, looping, studded with accusations.

"What's he look like?"

"I haven't seen the picture."

"A white guy."

"Middle-aged white guy."

"What's he doing here?"

"*Is* he here?"

"Wouldn't one of us know if he was?"

"Maybe one of us *does*."

Noreen, an elderly woman with bobbed hair who was an aunt of Clarence and Paula's, and godmother to many children in the valley, had been provided with a folding chair and was sitting next to Jocelyn on the step. "I have a doctor's appointment," she said. "Don't they know people have places to go?"

"My cell phone's not working," Clarence said. "But it usually doesn't work down here, so who knows? I just use my house phone when I'm at home."

"They could knock out the phones easily," Ron said. "The whole system is digital. They could switch off that tower like a light." There was a cell phone tower at the top of a hill half a mile away.

"No, no, my cell works," said Lena. "I called my mother. She said nobody's saying anything on the news yet." She opened her phone, rubbed the screen with her thumb, closed it again.

Livy's mother disengaged from her conversation with Jocelyn and came over to sit with Livy and Nelson on the step. She was laughing quietly, shaking her head. "Sometimes I don't know why we moved here," she said. "And then I remember what people were like the last place we lived. Guess it's the same all over."

"What's Jocelyn saying?" Livy asked.

"Jocelyn is the classic death-wisher. Jocelyn would be tickled to just see everything blow up."

"You think so?" Livy said. Nelson was listening intently. He had told Livy that he was amazed at the way her parents talked to her, mainly because of how much they cursed and how freely they slandered other adults.

"Oh yes, I do. And Ron," her mother said in a lower voice, watching the man gesturing a few feet away, tracing out shapes in the air, counting something off on his fingers. He had snared Livy's father in a conversation now, and Greg was standing back a couple of feet with his arms crossed, as if trying to stay out of range of Ron's overly expressive hands. "What a crackpot that guy is. He thinks the parks department is holding up his fishing license because of his political beliefs."

"What are his political beliefs?" Nelson ventured.

Livy's mother burst out laughing. "I encourage you to go ask him. He'll tell you all about it." But then she settled her features and looked away, and Livy understood the subject to be closed. This usually happened when people talked about Ron Cash—a statement of some unpleasant truth and then an embarrassed lapse into silence. This was because the Cashes were a tragic family. In fact, the word *tragic* was permanently linked with them in Livy's inner lexicon, because she had been only six when their son died, and it was the first time she had heard the word used out loud. Eric Cash had lived to be five. They used to bring him down to swim in the creek sometimes, so Livy had known him in a way, a pale kid always more closely watched than the others, bathed in an aura of nervous attention. He had been sick all his life, and died one summer in a hospital in Paoli.

The Cashes had always been aggressive neighbors with loud habits. But the death of their son created a strange bubble of silence around them. For a year or two after Eric died, people couldn't bear to speak ill of Ron no matter what he did, especially people who had children. They tolerated him, and showered his silent wife with strained attempts at friendliness. So Ron went unchecked. He made himself the king of a tiny kingdom, burning his trash instead of dragging it down to the road, setting up target practice in his backyard despite ordinances that forbade firing a weapon within three hundred yards of a dwelling. He burgeoned, also, with ideas, grand ordering ideas in which he and his wife were the focus of nefarious organizations and occult patterns, the narrowest point of a funnel of trouble, and no one argued with these ideas to his face, because wasn't he right, in a way? If you had suffered like that, shouldn't you feel free to consider yourself the center of a malevolent universe? Livy's mother was less tolerant than many, because she was half Jewish and his rants sometimes touched on the Jews. But even so, she often held her tongue.

Maurice Carden came jogging across the bridge and stopped at the edge of the little crowd, out of breath.

"They're going door to door on White Horse Road," he said. "I just saw them."

"Whose house?" said Clarence.

"All of them. They're at the Christmases' place already, I just saw them go in."

"They need a warrant," Ron said, shaking his head. He was rubbing his stiff knee with one hand, wincing.

"Maybe they have one," Clarence said.

A woman in sweatpants detached from the crowd and hurried toward the bridge. A few others who lived on White Horse Road followed her.

"Are they coming over here?" Noreen said.

"Probably," Maurice said.

The talk continued, but it was quieter now, and people's eyes kept drifting toward the bridge. Nelson dropped handfuls of fine gravel down the neck of his empty soda bottle. Livy perceived that he was leaning a little closer to her mother now, perhaps unconsciously, as if he were borrowing her in the absence of his own. The faint crackle of a walkie-talkie drifted down to them from White Horse Road.

When the police emerged from the trees at the far end of the bridge, the conversations in front of the store ceased entirely. There were five or six police officers there, in short-sleeved Maronne uniforms, on foot. They chatted with each other as they approached, talked into radios, peered over the sides of the bridge. Livy glanced at the neighbors standing in the intersection and was startled to see how they looked with their attention so united, so powerfully focused in one direction. For a moment they looked fierce, despite the men wearing bifocals and the women holding their hair off the backs of their sweaty necks.

"We're looking for this man," said the policeman in front as he reached the intersection. He held the large photo up in front of him. "Anybody seen him?"

"We don't know who that is," Noreen said.

"We have good reason to believe he's in the immediate area," said the policeman, holding the photo a little higher. The people leaning against the guardrail shouted questions.

"Who is he?"

"Is he dangerous?"

"Name is Ree-vaz Den-nee," said the policeman, reading from the back of the photo.

"Where's he from?"

"Europe, they said."

"He could be from lots of places. Lebanese people are white-looking sometimes," Jocelyn said, leaning toward Livy confidentially. "I used to live in Beckford."

Livy's mother snorted quietly. Jocelyn and Ron were launching into a taxonomy of whiteness, listing groups that were and groups that were not as if this would have to lead them eventually to the suspect's specific nationality, like a game of Guess Who? with all the tiles flipped down. Black neighbors nearby, Paula and Noreen in particular, rolled their eyes. The policeman lowered the photo slightly, unsure that he had their attention. "We're acting under direction from the federal level," he said.

"We're asking is he *dangerous* or not," Clarence said again.

"I have a doctor's appointment," Noreen called out, getting up from her chair.

"We can't open up the area until we've resolved it," said the policeman.

"She has an appointment!" Ron said. "This is an older woman, sir!"

"We're talking about an international issue, sir. We can't let anybody through. We don't have that kind of latitude."

A young-looking policeman came closer and tried to pass around another copy of the photo; there was a long pause before anyone would take it from his hand. *Revaz Deni* was printed at the bottom. When it was passed to Livy, she looked at the name, trying to summon any association at all—a country, a language—but nothing came to her.

"Maybe it's a joke," Nelson muttered. "An incredibly elaborate joke."

"We're going to have to ask you to return to your homes," said the policeman in front.

"How long is this going to be?" said Jocelyn. "What about the power? And the phones?"

"We really can't answer that at this time. The best thing for everybody right now is to go home. In all seriousness, folks."

Talk started up again, but the crowd began to disperse. Nelson's mother came around the corner, tremulous in a heavy beaded necklace and slacks, and picked her way through the crowd, obviously looking for her son. Livy watched her approach, not stirring herself to alert Nelson. Mrs. Tela never came down to the store, even if she was out of coffee or eggs. She would send Nelson or his sister Janine instead, and it was always with a dubious sigh and a fistful of crumpled singles, as if she weren't really confident that money could be exchanged for goods there in the conventional manner. The fact that she was here now showed how alarmed she must be over the police, enough to come down from her little house on the hillside to fetch her younger child. Mrs. Tela was the only snob Livy knew, which made her interesting. Livy knew that the store was grimy and low-rent; it was impossible not to notice the strips of flypaper, the missing acoustic tiles in the ceiling, the way the inventory never covered the shelf space. But Mrs. Tela was the only person she knew who seemed annoyed about it, as if it undermined the tenor of her life. She didn't like Nelson hanging around the intersection or the steps in front, believing (and here Livy had to admit that she wasn't entirely wrong) that it was a magnet for reprobates, a place where trouble was spontaneously generated. Livy watched her nod a few hellos and then catch sight of Nelson. "There you are," she said.

Nelson looked startled, and then stood up with a sigh, brushing the dust off the back of his pants. "See you later," he said to Livy.

✳

The searches took up the whole afternoon. Livy's parents told her to stay in the house, and her nervous energy propelled her up to her room and then through the hinged skylight onto the roof. It was too steep to be comfortable but she stayed there for a long time with her feet braced against the shingles, twisting apart maple seeds that had landed there, picking at the scabs on her legs. When she had destroyed all the loose vegetation within reach she went down into her bedroom for a bottle of nail polish and climbed up to sit on the chimney. Painting her nails was a default activity, something she did when her mind was disorderly and she had time to kill, which was a common condition for her in the summer. She had taught herself to do it, since she had no sisters and her mother owned no cosmetics. Cosmetics were among the many ordinary things her parents had no patience for. Greg and Mariel Marko belonged to no clubs, leagues, teams, or religious groups, and there was a long and diverse list of books they would not read, foods they would not eat, clothing they would not wear, TV shows they would not watch, and music they would not listen to. Livy had absorbed the logic of this list at such a young age that she could apply it at will, but it would have been very difficult, at sixteen, to explain it to someone else. In broad terms, the items on this list of prohibitions were all either violent, extravagant, very popular, or filled with chemicals, and sometimes some combination of the four.

Her parents had a collection of old-world skills between them: they could frame out a house, raise

chickens and goats, make butter and cheese and yo-
gurt. Her mother could knit, sew, bake bread, repair
fences, overpower the morbidity of a broody hen. They
knew how to do these things because they had gone
back to the land before Livy was born. They'd lived in
a cabin they built together, forgoing running water and
electricity, basking in a total lack of other people to
bother them. They'd owned a cow named Angeline;
there were pictures of her in the family photo album.
They had lived more or less without jobs, and this was a
point that caught Livy's attention now that she was old
enough to have a job herself. Jobs were awful; bosses
were awful. They talked to you like you were stupid.
She came home from her shifts at the restaurant sometimes and complained over dinner about these facts,
and her parents were completely in agreement. Other
people *were* awful: they did talk to you like you were
stupid, and a lot of the time they were actually the ones
who were stupid, and there was no way around this
situation that Livy's parents could suggest except a
total withdrawal from the world. They'd had to come
back from the land, of course, after a few years. Her
father said, frankly, that it had gotten too hard and they
were tired. They'd had a winter of record-breaking cold,
and they couldn't keep enough dry wood in the cabin
to stay warm, and they'd decided to move back to the

eastern side of the state and have a baby. That was when they moved to Lomath, and a year later Livy was born.

They had transmitted to her, in addition to a dislike of jobs, a kind of bodily discomfort in the presence of the police, which Livy had never fully considered the strangeness of until now. She remembered that once, years ago when she was eight or nine years old, a black-and-white police cruiser came down the long driveway that the Markos shared with the neighbors, creeping along with gravel popping under the tires, and made a slow three-point turn in the little muddy lot in front of the mill. Livy had stood with her mother just where their own private driveway joined the shared one, watching the cruiser go by, waiting until it was finally gone. Why were they out there? What were they expecting would happen? She couldn't remember. A sense of anxiety adhered to the memory. It seemed odd now, inexplicable, looking back. Her parents were cranks, but they were also middle-aged people with jobs. They liked to imagine that they were a threat to the social order; maybe that was all.

Around three o'clock she saw the police come around the bend of the low road on foot and knock on the Greens' door. The Greens came out and stood in the yard while the police filed in. Livy watched while two officers circled the house and disappeared into the backyard. The Greens stood in the driveway for a while, under the eye of the policeman at the door, and then sat down one by one in the grass under the windbreak of lindens they had planted along the road. Livy watched nervously. Clarence and Aurelia Green were also middle-aged people with jobs, just like the Markos, but they were black, and she was old enough to grasp that it made a difference. In Maronne, where most of the police department was white and most of the people were not, she had seen beat cops walk up to groups of men and women chatting on the sidewalk and tell them to "disperse," the specificity of the word carrying an air of statute. This was called "clearing the sidewalk," and it came up sometimes in city council meetings when people complained. Livy finished painting her toenails while she watched the Greens sitting in their yard, and then she painted her fingernails, and then colored the stone between her feet sparkly blue. She had painted a good deal of the masonry within reach of her left hand by the time the police came out of the Green house again and picked their way up the hill to the Cardens'. The Greens went back inside, Clarence and Aurelia ushering their twin girls ahead of them, and Livy heard the faint, abbreviated bang of their front door closing from across the creek.

She heard the porch door open below her, and her father stepped down onto the grass beside the ash tree and paused, looking in every direction. It was funny to see people foreshortened this way, all crown with little wobbling bodies underneath, like toddlers. "Hey," she called down.

He started and looked up, peering through his glasses. She waved.

"What are you doing up there?" he said. He sounded angry.

"I won't fall off," she offered. "I've got three points of contact." With one hand she indicated her feet, firmly planted on the copper flashing, and her other hand, resting on the stones.

"You fall off and hit the porch roof, you'll break your leg," he said.

He was glaring as if she were doing something outrageous, absurd. She was confused, which made her annoyed in turn. "You never fussed about me going on the roof before," she said.

"Christ, just get off the chimney," he said. "Stay over on the side. At least if you fall off you'll hit the grass."

"Okay, all right," she said, climbing down onto the shingles. She heard the door shut as he went back inside. She guessed he was on edge about the police, and taking it out on her. He did not normally object to heights, and he was the one who had chosen a fully opening skylight to install in her room instead of the hobbled kind that stopped at a few inches, admitting nothing but bugs. Incidents like this one made her notice how lax her parents were with her the rest of the time: the driving around late at night and talking back and sleeping over wherever she wanted. Her classmates in college-bound classes at school, all of them nonthreatening, polite kids whom teachers and administrators happily ignored, were not allowed to do these things.

Some time later Livy came down off the roof to make herself a piece of toast, and the house was filled with scorching bleach fumes. She found her mother in the kitchen levering dirt out of the cracks between the floorboards with a butter knife. Her father was scrubbing the walls in the living room, and small showers of flakes were coming loose from a patch of water-damaged plaster near the chimney, clinging to his hair and beard, whitening the Harbor County Auto Fair T-shirt he'd put on for the chore.

"I've been meaning to do this," Livy's mother said as she came in. She was wiping the black material lifted from the cracks onto a piece of paper towel. Her hair was coming loose from a bun, and there was a sheen over her that Livy guessed was some combination of anxiety and heat.

"You're all red," Livy said.

"That's a nice thing to say to your old mother," she said. "You are also all red, for the record."

"Are you worried?" Livy said. "Is that why you're doing this?" The fumes made her throat constrict. She wanted them to admit to some anxiety; she felt a little abandoned by their fierce activity.

"Why don't you get a broom and clear the spiders out of your room?" her father called from the other room. "I was up there yesterday and it was ridiculous. You like living with spiders?"

"They eat the millipedes," Livy said. She cut two slices of bread and put them in the toaster, and then stared at it before remembering the power was out. She took a frying pan from a nail on the wall instead.

"Are you saying you're not going to do it?" her father said. He was looking into the kitchen now from the living room. Livy's mother's back was to her, but she thought she saw a look pass between her parents. They seemed to have decided she was a problem, all of a sudden. It was one of those days.

"No, I'll do it," Livy said, placing the bread in the pan.

"You'd rather stay on the roof all afternoon?" her mother said.

When had the roof become a fight? Her mother and father were both watching her now. This always seemed to happen lately, contested territory cropping up in normal conversations. Livy was aware that she was to blame for some of this at times, that she defended her little patches of righteousness with the same vigor they did. But this one had caught her off guard.

"You're not a guest, you know," her mother said, pointing in the direction of the stairs with the dirt-laden butter knife. "You live here. You never clean."

"What? I clean—"

"You act so put-upon when I tell you to take your things up to your room or sweep out the basement. I ask you for *nothing*. And right now what we're asking is for you to clean your room this afternoon and stay the *hell off the roof.*"

Livy was speechless. Her mother was giving her a wide-eyed stare now, waiting for a response. Her father had a similar look. Livy turned off the flame under the pan.

"Okay," she said quietly.

"In your room with the skylight shut," her mother said. "Until we say otherwise. All right?"

"All right," Livy said. She was staring at her hands now, holding the two barely warmed slices of bread. She had to push past her father to get through the kitchen door, and he stepped aside and looked the other way, as if he had just noticed a crack in the plaster beside the south-facing window.

She sat on the floor in her room. A new grasp of the situation was dawning on her. It was an emergency, the kind that seeped into people's homes like radon poisoning and made them act peculiar: large, illogical animal-parents, eyes rolling in panic.

She heard murmuring in the kitchen, and then the house was quiet. She cleaned. She swept the corners, cleared the loose objects off her desk and dresser, took her books out of the shelves and wiped the dust off their tops with a paper towel. She filled a trash bag with plastic odds and ends whose provenance she could no longer remember and Christmas-gift knickknacks she didn't want, and spent an hour leafing through the old magazines stacked in the closet, feeding them one by one into a recycling bag. They were evidence of a cheerfully standard femininity she had passed through at fourteen, when she had decided there might not be any good reason she shouldn't know techniques for flat-ironing her hair or "creating a waist" or giving herself a "smoky eye." The magazines had gradually infuriated her with their chummy, innocent tone and constant faultfinding, and now she was firmly against them, but she could still be drawn in by the sticky perfume samples and the photographs of beautiful girls in oversized sweaters, walking in grassy fields at sunset, with dabs of lens flare above their backlit hair. Nelson had found the magazines once while searching for an extra sweatshirt in her closet, and then read an article on "taming flyaways" out loud to her with great seriousness. The illustrating pictures were not clear enough for him to grasp what a flyaway was, and he was apparently struck by the lyricism of the phrase, because he tried to deduce it through a series of questions.

"It's not a knot," he said.

"No," she said.

"It's not a cowlick."

"No."

"So it's little hairs just sticking straight up," he said. "Like they're trying to *fly away* from the rest of your hair."

"Yes."

"Like if you have static electricity?"

"No. Yes. Sometimes."

She leafed through the magazines in the quiet house. When they were tied up inside the bag she lay down and slept, trying to will the time away.

❋

It was evening by the time the police knocked on the Markos' door, explaining that the search was voluntary pending a warrant but that it would make everything go much faster if they consented to it. The Markos went out to stand in the yard, leaving the gleaming, bleach-scented house to be searched by several tired-looking men in button-front shirts and dark pants. A young female police officer stood with them in the yard, smiling apologetically. Livy's father chatted with her the way he chatted with grocery clerks, perhaps to soothe his anxiety.

The sound of heavy furniture scraping across the floor came to them through the screened front door. Livy's mother winced, which the policewoman noticed. "Most places, they put everything back the way they found it," she said.

"You really can't tell us anything about this person?" her father said.

"There are just a lot of security concerns," the young woman said, pressing her lips together.

※

Nelson knocked on the Markos' kitchen door softly, with two knuckles. Livy was standing at the stove, making hot chocolate. It was inappropriate for the season but the stove was the only appliance in the house that worked the same with or without electricity, and it was soothing to use it. The kitchen had been left mostly undisturbed in the search; some things had been pulled out of closets upstairs, and the beer cases and sacks of lime in the basement had been moved away from the walls, but that was all.

"Your mom let you out?" Livy said, as Nelson maneuvered around the counter and sat at the table. Livy was wearing a pair of cotton shorts that were too small to be seen in outside the house, and she would have been self-conscious about them if not for the darkness of the candlelit kitchen. They revealed the white of her upper thighs where normal shorts covered them, the faint blue veins, the dark sideways hairs that she didn't bother to go after with a razor.

"She's been asleep since eight," Nelson said.

Livy glanced up at the battery-operated clock on the wall. It was eleven thirty. Her own parents had gone to sleep at ten, looking run-down, hardly saying good night.

"She's been in bed since this afternoon." He picked up the saltshaker, rolled it back and forth along its edge on the surface of the table.

"Is she acting weird?" Livy said, turning to watch him answer. Livy had once seen Nelson's mother throw a candlestick through a picture window. "Acting weird" was a code phrase they had used for years to refer to his mother's problem: the fact that she sometimes wouldn't get out of bed for days and seemed both blind and deaf to people who came into her bedroom to try to make her eat, and that when pressed, in that state, she could inflict astonishing violence on the inside of the house. She broke plates and put holes in the drywall. She had knocked Nelson down a few times.

"Yeah, she's getting weird," Nelson said. He was picking at the holes in the top of the saltshaker with his thumbnail.

"Okay," Livy said. "We can play checkers."

Livy's room was a loft, open to the kitchen below on one side. The Marko house was tall and narrow and regular as a cake, three small stories stacked on top of each other, built into the side of the hill so it had front doors on two different levels. There were few interior doors, and a quiet knock on the kitchen door was plainly audible in Livy's room, though it would not carry into the master bedroom where her parents slept. Their room was on the ground floor, half underground, and had a heavy door. Nelson had been coming and going from the Marko house at night for years without disturbing her parents.

When they were thirteen and fourteen Nelson would tell Livy at school that his mother was acting weird, and Livy would understand that she should take the cordless phone with her when she went to bed in case he called in the middle of the night to come over. Livy would bring the cushions from the living room couch up to her room and arrange them on the floor for him to sleep on. He was electrified with tension and fatigue when he appeared at those times, so much so that he would whisper jokes the whole time, sexual jokes, which was not normal for him—filling the late-night silence with innuendoes about sharing a room, treating the whole thing as a ruse by her to get him alone, or the other way around. Livy had been surprised the first time by this bewildering edifice of just-kidding, but she had learned that he wouldn't refer to it later and everything would be back to normal the next day. So she played along, insinuating back at him. She enjoyed those times, even though they were bad times. They were bubbles of intimacy that appeared and then vanished and left everything just as it had been before. He would sleep a few hours and then get up before dawn to put the cushions back and slip away to his own house. Livy's parents never knew.

Around the time they turned fifteen, he stopped making late-night rescue calls. Livy suspected that he had learned to be embarrassed.

She finished the hot chocolate and made a cup for him too, and they went looking for the checkers set. It was missing a third of its pieces, so they found a pack of cards instead and played by candlelight in the middle of Livy's bedroom floor. Through the open windows they could hear occasional sirens over the hills. There was a fire station in Parna that had a government-grade siren, an enormous aluminum concavity under a little shingled belfry roof, and it went off frequently in the summer. It meant there was a fire that needed extra trucks in one of the neighboring townships, and despite its hysterical pitch it frightened neither of them.

"Aces low," Livy said.

"You didn't say that before."

"Come on." She made a give-me-a-break gesture, palms up.

"You didn't," he said, laughing. "You are such a cheater. This is why I don't trust your line calls."

"You can't see my line calls." They sometimes played badminton on the sandy lot in front of the mill when they got tired of watching pirated movies in the dark, and he always took off his glasses to play, which led to a lot of disputes about what was out of bounds. The sand and the net were there because the carpenters who owned the mill met once a week to play volleyball and drink beer on the mosquito-livened lawn. They had even set up lights on tall rusted poles so they could play after dark. When she was little, Livy and the other carpenters' kids would play a parallel game on those evenings, a literal shadow game, in which each child picked an adult shadow and strived to stay in it while it moved up and down the court.

"Cheating a blind man at badminton," Nelson said, shaking his head.

Livy laughed. "You could always keep your glasses on." She put down a nine of hearts, and Nelson reconsidered his hand. "Doesn't this feel like camping?" she said, watching him stare at the four cards he held. "That's the only time I do boring things like this. Cards, for God's sake." She thought boredom was definitely the way to go, if they were going to be discussing their feelings. There was a certain bravado to it.

"Camping or a long car trip," Nelson said. "Or a train ride. Or the guy in the bubble over Times Square for a week." He scratched his chin. "Those Russian soldiers who were trapped in the submarine."

"They all died, Nelson, it's not quite like that."

"How long do you think it'll be?" he said. He was studying his cards.

"I don't know," Livy said.

"Let's do bets, though." He glanced up. His glasses were sliding down his nose, and he pushed them up. "Over-under."

"Hmm." She studied the ceiling. "Tomorrow morning. Before noon."

He nodded, looking at his cards again. "That's optimistic."

"Well, they've already searched most of the houses and they haven't found anybody. So they have to go soon, right?"

"But maybe it's the opposite," he said. "They haven't found him, so they can't leave."

She thought about that. "So you want to take after-noon."

"Yeah. They leave before noon, you win. They leave after noon, I win."

"So if things are okay, then I win, and if everything is terrible, then you win," Livy said.

Nelson laughed. "I guess that's my system, yeah."

"It's not going to take that long," Livy said, trying briefly to push her voice into a tone that was serious and reassuring. She was thinking of his mother again. "It'll be all right."

"Hm." He laid down a jack of diamonds. It was an indifferent play. The sirens stopped, started, stopped again.

At one o'clock they exhausted the deck and he stood up to go. He patted his pockets absently, making sure he had his keys; delaying, shifting his weight. He went over to the skylight and looked out, as if he would be able to assess the circumstances at his own house from there.

"You don't have to go," Livy said.

He turned quickly and she regretted it for an instant, as if she'd accidentally used an obscenity in a foreign lan-guage. "I don't mean it in a weird way," she said, but that made it worse. There was a glare on his glasses from the candle, and she couldn't tell if he was staring at her or not. "You know what I mean. You used to."

"I used to be more scared," he said.

"You're not scared now?"

He rubbed his nose and glanced out the skylight again. "I used to be smaller," he said.

She was appalled. "You don't have to go."

"Thanks," he said. He sounded sincere.

"It's fine if you do," Livy said. "But you don't have to."

He brushed his fingers over the top of her head, just barely disturbing her hair, and she started but did not move back. "Thanks," he said again.

She watched him go down the stairs, and heard the kitchen door open and close; it would lock automatically behind him. She thought about the phones being down; he couldn't call. She hoped everything was quiet when he got home.

She was sitting opposite a mirror that leaned against the wall, and when she glanced at it she saw that her shirt had come down in front while she was hunched on the floor, and the edge of her bra was visible. It occurred to her that Nelson had been sitting right in front of the mirror, and it was likely that she had been chatting with him and playing cards while giving him a clear view down the front of her shirt. That was embarrassing. She pulled the shirt back up, but it was old and had been washed too many times and didn't lie flat against her skin anyway. She edged up to the mirror on her knees and stared herself in the eyes, recalling how easy it had been to give herself vertigo that way when she was a child. She looked all right. She looked kind of nice in the candlelight.

Nelson had had a nervous, humorless girlfriend when he was fifteen, an eleventh grader with her own car who'd had sex with him in it after stopping at his house on her way home from a field hockey meet. She wasn't nice to him, and she wouldn't let him talk to Livy. They'd broken up after three months. Livy was still a virgin. She had pressed Nelson for sexual details, but he'd turned red and said nothing.

"So everything, then," she had said.

He was pink all the way to the roots of his hair. "Not—no. Not everything."

"But you *did*—"

"Yeah. But that's, you know. Not everything."

She was annoyed that he wouldn't tell her more, but she could also see that he was being decent. She felt a little left out.

"You'd tell me if I was a boy," she said.

"No, I wouldn't," he said.

She abandoned the mirror and went to bed without brushing her teeth. She was too keyed up to fall asleep. She was listening for people moving in the dark, the police or the man they were looking for, or anything else. How did she not listen every night? How was it that a person could feel so safe, so much of the time?

⁂

Revaz was settling in for an uncomfortable night. The woods were full of mosquitoes, and they seemed even thicker in the deer blind, attracted by the heat it trapped, maybe, or the old sour smells of the wood. He had come to the conclusion that animals had lived in the blind since its last human use. That would explain the rancid, biological liveliness of it. He was a city dweller and had never had romantic ideas about nature. He had not slept in the open since he was a boy.

He had been expecting his old friend Davit's cousin that day, the one who drove a truck for a living. That was the plan: after flying into Philadelphia and taking the commuter train out to Lomath, he would meet Davit's cousin on the highway over the hill. Then they would drive west. He was not sure how far he would go with the cousin; he was simply anxious to get far away from the airport. On the highways a person could disappear. He understood that in this spectacular run of favors he had used up his friendship with Davit, burned it out like a candle.

Just after dawn that morning he had walked down out of the woods to the bleached and neglected-looking road that ran along the creek, and after going the wrong way for ten minutes he had made it to Prospect Road, intending to climb up to the rendezvous point on the highway that Davit had marked for him on the map. He saw the police cruiser at Somersburg Road before the policeman in it saw him, and was able to climb over the guardrail and retreat undetected. This was good luck, although it had crossed his mind, for a few brief minutes while he tried to catch his breath on a rock beside the creek, that he might have been spared arrest only to die of a heart attack. He was already faint from hunger, and the shock of seeing the police car made his heart race horribly. The rush of adrenaline made him sweat, too: his shirt, creased and dirty from sleeping on benches and train platforms and finally in the deer blind, was now marked with dark circles under both arms and a damp plume down the back.

He had brought an empty plastic water bottle with him, and he had the presence of mind to fill it in the creek before he headed back. The thing was that the less you had, the harder it was to get anything. The light-headedness of hunger made this seem very profound. He had nothing. After paying off the cousin through Davit and buying his plane ticket, he had $232 in cash left in the world. He was afraid to try buying something to eat. And buy it where? He had a cell phone, a pay-as-you-go that he'd bought in Philadelphia before he got on the train so that he could call the cousin—a number that he had committed to memory, not wanting it to be found on him in case he was arrested—but if the police were here then they might be monitoring cell phone calls coming out of the area. And sometimes phones had GPS trackers in them, didn't they? He took the phone out of his pocket and stared at it for several minutes, trying to remember how the chips worked from spy movies he'd seen on television. Finally he risked a single text message, not identifying himself by name, hoping that the cousin would deduce who he was from the language: *Delayed, try tomorrow.* Then he took the battery out of the phone and put both in his pocket.

Back in the deer blind, his heart beating at close to normal pace again, it occurred to him that the police car might have nothing to do with him. It was possible. He nodded to himself, crouched on the platform a mere six feet off the ground. Possible, but a useless possibility, too risky to act on. He drank the water, and his headache receded a little. He worried about parasites. There might be cows shitting in the stream, for all he knew. He had seen some on the hillside at the far end of the valley.

He had no idea what to do. He was able to fall asleep for a while, though the sun was high and it was hot in the blind. Hunger woke him close to noon, and he climbed down out of the tree and took a piss in a clump of bushes a few feet away—some decorum, even if he was alone. A baby's changing table stuck out of a blackberry bush nearby, its wood panels warped and delaminated from exposure.

He chewed experimentally on some grass in an especially succulent-looking clump, and was shocked to discover that it tasted like onions. It made his mouth burn but it was comforting to have the scent on his breath—it was homey and he thought of dumplings. It tempered, also, the bitter empty-stomach taste of his saliva. He investigated the blackberry bush, but it was well past the season. The crevices in the bedrock that reared up out of the top of the ridge were filled with rotting walnuts, golfball–sized green globes that flaked to black, but he had no idea if they would make him sick if he ate them raw. From the top of the bedrock he could catch glimpses of a long view through the trees: the farm at the top of the valley, the sweep of the ridge opposite, the white house with the garden directly below him.

There was a person sitting on the chimney of the white house. A woman or girl, probably, with long hair. She was crouched there like a gargoyle, absorbed.

He watched her for a little while, discerning the open hatch in the roof that she had apparently come through. He was unsettled by the sight of her in a way he couldn't name.

Then he saw the police on the road below him. One was in uniform and the rest were not, but it was clear they were police: two were talking into radios. They ambled from the road toward a house at the bottom of the same slope he perched on, a house mostly hidden from him by the trees. He ran for the safety of the deer blind. He felt his leg scrape on something as he climbed the boards nailed to the trunk of the tree. He collapsed against the front wall of the blind and checked his leg: he'd torn his cuff, and he was bleeding a little from a spot just beside his Achilles tendon. He must have gotten caught on a nail. He untucked his shirt and wiped his sweating forehead with the tail. He understood now why he'd been disturbed at the sight of the girl on the chimney: she had been keeping vigil, and it was the police she was watching for. What were these people thinking, as the police hemmed them in? It made him dizzy to imagine it. What a great distance there was between them and himself, and yet here they all were.

✳

The next morning Livy got out of the house with the excuse of fetching bread from the store. They were down to a single curving heel-end. It was cloudy that morning, the birds hushed. The OPEN flag hung limply by the door, half covering the Dempsey Market sign. Livy was relieved to see it. She had been thinking that Jocelyn might stay closed, given the lockdown, and retreat to her apartment upstairs.

Years ago, when Livy was small, it was Noreen who owned and operated the store. The neighborhood children lived their summer hours in an orbit between the creek and the store, and Noreen was Aunt Noreen to most of them. It was delightful to children to be able to walk to a place of business and make purchases. They fetched milk and eggs for their mothers, and spent their allowances on penny candy and ice cream bars. When Noreen felt she was too old, she sold it to Jocelyn, who kept it much the same—the same freezer cases, pinball machine, occasional yard-sale items along the windowsills—but filled it with a nervous energy that Noreen had never had. Jocelyn talked fast and smoked on the steps, and she smiled at the kids a lot in a way that suggested she was afraid they might not like her. Still, her store was the place where people went when they wanted to get out of the house for a minute. They went barefoot, sometimes, or in bathrobes.

Noreen was sitting in her honorary position in a folding chair just inside the door and keeping up a half-shouted conversation with Jocelyn, who stood ten feet away behind the counter. Shelly Cash was picking her nails in a corner.

"I told those boys not to sit out there," Noreen yelled hoarsely. "I used to chase them away when they tried it. But you let them sit there."

"I tell them to go," Jocelyn said. "They just don't listen to me."

"Well, you have to make them listen to you."

Jocelyn seemed tense. Livy guessed they were talking about Brian and Dominic and some of their friends, who liked to sit on the front steps and smoke. It was true that Noreen had not tolerated this kind of thing when she owned the store, but it was also true that there had been a different set of teenage boys then.

"Morning, Noreen," Livy said.

"Livy!" Noreen said. She leaned over and patted Livy's knee. "You're a good girl. How'd you do in school this year?"

"Okay, pretty good."

"All right. You stay focused. That's really what it's about, don't you think, Jocelyn?"

"Mm-hmm," Jocelyn said. Her shoulders were always up lately and her head was always down, her hair in a long swinging ponytail that seemed too lighthearted for her. She was smoking, which she did not ordinarily do inside the store.

Noreen shook her head. "Just keep an eye on your friends. You are the company you keep."

Livy smiled politely. The bells rattled on the door, and Angela Insky came in. She was wearing a man's work shirt and boots, and her gray hair was falling out of a topknot. "There are a couple of plainclothes cops watching the highway right behind my house," she announced. "I've been watching out my window all morning."

"What kind of cops?" Noreen said, putting her hand to her ear.

"PLAINCLOTHES COPS!" Angela thundered helpfully, pivoting toward her. Livy snorted into her hand, and then pretended to be comparing the nutrition labels on two loaves of bread.

"How do you know they're cops, then?" Jocelyn said.

"You think civilians are surveilling my house?" Angela said.

Livy edged around Angela with a loaf of bread and a newspaper from the rack. Jocelyn glanced over her items. "Paper's free. It's two days old."

Livy paid for the bread and went out on the steps to read the comics. She didn't want to go home yet. Lena and Paula arrived, and Livy half listened to their conversation through the propped door.

"Let's think about this logically," Lena said. "Who would hide somebody from the police? There are some people who would and some people who wouldn't."

"You don't know anybody's hiding him at all," Paula said. "Even if he is here, which I have my doubts about, and Tobias has his doubts about." Tobias was her live-in boyfriend of many years, a cop, who had been on an overnight shift when the roads were blocked off and had not been able to come home. There were a few other halves of couples stuck outside Lomath now—stranded night-shift workers, now sleeping on the couches of relatives nearby—but Paula's case warranted special attention, since her boyfriend had been coming up to the barricades now and then to give her bits of information.

"You talked to him?" Noreen said.

"A little bit. He says it's a mess."

"Is that all?"

"He said there's a bunch of FBI guys taking over the station house. They took his fax machine. And now they're trying to send him up to Springton Manor to sit in a speed trap all day because they don't like him coming by to talk to me. He said they're trying to keep their plans a secret but he thinks there isn't any plan."

"Was it them that shut off the power?" Lena said.

"Looks like it was. And the phones."

Jocelyn sighed. "Who do you think would do it, though?" she said. "Hide somebody?"

"I'll tell you who wouldn't," Lena said. "Clarence and Aurelia. Noreen. Paula." She nodded toward her friend.

"What makes you so sure?" Paula said.

"Oh, don't make jokes," Lena said. "It could be one of those war criminals from Sarajevo, those snipers who were shooting little children. You remember that? Schoolkids running across a bridge."

"That's not the Balkans. That's Bosnia," Paula said.

"Bosnia is *in* the Balkans."

Paula frowned. "It is? Well, I guess I don't remember. That was forever ago."

"I don't think we need to speculate," Noreen said. She had a slightly mournful tone that Livy thought she'd heard before, in her own grandparents' voices, when an old fight was getting started again at the dinner table. It must be so tiring to be old enough to know better than everybody. Livy gave up trying to read the paper and leaned in the doorway to listen.

"I wouldn't hide anybody the police were looking for," Lena said. "My son, *maybe*."

"I don't think anybody's here at all," said Shelly Cash suddenly. She had long, freckled hands, and she was drawing M&M's out of a packet one by one, rolling them in her palm before she ate them. She barely moved her lips when she spoke, but her voice always cut clear through the air. She was both larger and smaller than life, physically reduced but unsettling to others, every face turning toward her at the slightest sound. "They're just trying to look like they're doing their job. Which means making us look like criminals while they're at it, and if I don't get to work by Thursday I'm going to get fired."

"They don't care," Jocelyn concurred. "When Jeremiah got arrested he stepped on somebody's foot by accident, and they put him down for assault on a police officer. He already had the cuffs on. They don't care."

Livy stored this tidbit away, thinking she would tell Nelson about it later. Jeremiah's explanations for his problems always followed this pattern. Innocent act piled on innocent act, with inexplicable malice from teachers and security guards and police at every step. They'd had the same gym class when Livy was a freshman and Jeremiah was a junior, and she had heard him go on this way many times.

"Where is Jeremiah?" Lena said.

There was some interest in this question. Jocelyn looked sharply at Lena. "He's been with his dad in Panoke since June," she said. She turned away and started tying up the bag in the trash can behind her.

"Lucky for him," said Paula lightly.

Jocelyn walked around the counter with the trash bag, her face tight with anger. No insinuation about her son escaped her notice.

"Sweetheart," Noreen said, "I don't think they're going to come pick that up tonight."

Jocelyn stopped, and then walked back around the counter and pushed the full bag back into a corner by a pile of delivery boxes. There was a tight, thwarted silence. Lena Spellar noisily removed a piece of nicotine gum from a bubble pack. Livy pretended to study her newspaper again. The newsprint felt antique already between her fingers, brittle, coated with dust.

Clarence Green drove up from the low road in his big conversion van. Livy watched while he pulled up in front of the store and parked conscientiously, getting as close to the steps as possible, even though he could have left the van in the middle of the intersection if he'd wanted. He left the engine idling and stepped out.

"They're talking about it on the radio," he called out.

"No shit?" Jocelyn said. Paula pushed past her and ran outside. Noreen took longer. The radio voice surged out of the car. It was one of the Philadelphia stations, an anchorwoman whose voice was familiar, though Livy couldn't remember her name.

"—Interpol reports," the anchorwoman said. "Details are still sketchy. The FBI has issued no statement."

"What did she say?" cried Noreen, blinking in the sunlight.

"Shhh, shhh," Clarence said.

"For now, roads remain closed in this small community." Then the station ID, a commercial break.

"What the hell!" cried Paula. "That was no information at all!"

"She said something about extradition before I got up here," Clarence said. He was out of breath. "I was just sitting in my driveway listening to the radio and they started saying how there's a roadblock but nobody's making any statements about it, and nobody knows anything. And that was about it."

"Well, leave it on," Paula said. "Maybe they'll come back to it."

Noreen went back into the store and dragged out her folding chair. The news anchors talked about car wrecks and flooding in the Midwest and bond trading and the weather. Noreen was anxious, leaning forward in her chair, and Livy could hear her breathing, light and rasping. By the time the news had cycled back around again and the same bits of information had been repeated, Livy couldn't stand to sit there anymore. She excused herself and walked away up the hill.

Nelson's sister opened the door and squinted hard into the sunlight. "Oh, it's you," she said. "Nelson, Livy's here." She pulled the door open another foot and padded away into the dark.

It was hot inside. The house was in the sun all the time; there were no shade trees on the harsh slope of the lawn. Livy tried to run her hands through the damp knots in her hair.

Nelson was asleep in his room. It was hotter than the hallway, hotter than the living room. The window was open but no air moved through the screen. The bed was stripped except for a fitted sheet and he was asleep in his underwear, on his back, with his arms and legs thrown out. She stopped in the doorway and then crossed the room quickly and shook him.

"What, what," he said. He shaded his eyes with his hand.

"You should close the window."

"It'll—make it hotter . . ."

"It could not possibly get any hotter in here."

He sat up, rubbing his face. Her eyes dropped to his back and then she stepped away and pretended to look out the window. He really didn't seem to notice when he was half-dressed around her. She had been carefully covering up, stripping to a bathing suit only when she was just about to get in the water, for years.

"I was having fucked-up dreams," he said.

She glanced at him. His hair was damp at his temples and the wrinkles of the sheet were printed into the skin of his shoulders.

"I was in all this mud." He stood up and pulled on his shirt and then sat down and slowly worked his legs

into a pair of swim trunks. "People were chasing me." He
stood up and put his arms around her.

She was startled. "Hey, what?" His face was hot
against her ear.

"What yourself," he said. "I had a nightmare." He
squeezed her and let go. "Let's go for a walk. I have to
get out of this house."

She took a second to follow him, still feeling the hot
pressure of his arm on hers. He went ahead of her into
the yard, toward the woods. Downhill two children were
playing in the drainage ditch at the side of the road—a
pretty little brook, pebbled and bright, despite the cor-
rugated pipes that swallowed it here and there. They were
shy, curly-haired children whom Livy had often seen, and
now as always they straightened up at the sight of teenagers and hid their sticks and bunches of weeds behind
their backs. They were too young to know that their ritu-
als were easy to guess, being common among children
who live near water. Livy had played like that once, nam-
ing and building, day after day. She had tried, once or
twice, to explain to Nelson how she had felt when she
first started visiting the Inskys' pastures at the other end
of the valley. She was nine, alone, and had picked her way
across the creek on a whim, committing herself to a long
and arduous navigation of the apron of nettles and thistles
that edged the bottom pasture. As soon as she had gotten

through this marshy patch and into the broad lap of the
farm, where she could walk without looking down at her
feet, she had felt a stunning freedom. A clear spring ran
before her, crowded with cattails; past an electric fence, a
hill rose gently to the horizon, interrupted halfway up by
a palisade of bedrock. On the close-cropped, grassy slope,
three tall old pear trees leaned close together. The ground
around their roots was littered with hard, speckled fruit.
So: there was water and food, and cleared land bordered
by a wilderness (the bedrock, covered with brambles and
poison ivy), which meant that to a nine-year-old's mind,
conditioned by dollhouses and dioramas, this farm was a
scale model of a whole country. It was a miniature new
continent, and Livy was gloriously alone in it, with mud
leaking into her shoes and ecstatic greed in her heart. She
gave everything names, declared herself empress, and
built a ritual around her daily entry, making up violent
rhymes to block the path of anyone trying to follow her.
*If you pass the reeds so high / You'll fall in a hole and die. /
Try to cross the little spring / Burn to death with nettle stings.*
She had stopped going in the winter, and when she came
back in the spring it was not the same. It must have been
some change in herself, but the sod was just sod now.

Nelson snapped a branch off a little dead tree as they
entered the path and swung it in the air in front of him,
pushing back a rope of brambles. A few yards into the

woods they headed right, up the slope. "I like this spot," Nelson said. Livy recognized it. She couldn't remember when she'd been there, but she recognized the tree, an old silvery beech leaning back and throwing up its limbs, charred by a lightning strike many years previous that had emptied it out at the bottom but left it alive. She remembered sitting inside it some afternoon when she was small.

"They were talking about us on the radio," she said.

"They were?" He settled down beside the tree and leaned back, his face relaxing slightly.

"They didn't really say anything new. Just that they're looking for somebody and the roads are closed. Somebody foreign." She looked up into the leaves of the tree. "I mean, they didn't say that. They said something about extradition."

"That was it?"

She nodded and sat down beside him, glancing at the side of his face. His eyes were wide and dark, looking off into the trees.

"You know, I had something compressing when the power went out," he said. "I think I lost it."

"What was it?"

"The video with the ants." He had a cheap video camera and he'd been recording an anthill at the side of his driveway, an impressive structure, the ground humped and delicate beneath, the ants glinting red. There was a song he'd put with it, several songs; he kept trying them and discarding them, and there was something endearing about this, his focus on a project whose parameters were clear only to him, his emphatic rejection of one song, the hopeful way he took up another. Crouching for an hour at a time next to a mound of dirt, ducking around the side of the house when his parents or sister came outside.

"Did you have it backed up?" Livy said.

"I can't remember. I keep trying to remember, and I can't."

"I bet you did. You're always careful about that," she said. He looked like he was reviewing it in his mind, the video that might or might not exist now in the silent lump of his hard drive. She thought of elaborating a bit more on this reassuring idea, but decided not to. Sometimes she blundered too loudly into these private spaces in his life, his projects, his machinations, and she could feel him cringe.

There was a platform in a tree about ten yards away, between the edge of the Telas' yard and where they sat, that some kids had nailed up many years before. It was a pallet braced across two low branches and covered with a rotting carpet. When she was a kid she and her friends had sometimes used this tree for a game called Desert Island: the platform was the island, and the ground was a shark-infested sea, and they had nothing to eat and were alone in the world. Livy could just see the dark shape of it through the leaves. "Do you think that story about Jeremiah is true?" she said.

"Yeah, maybe," Nelson said. During the previous winter three men had robbed a bar at gunpoint in Maronne and some people said that Jeremiah, Jocelyn's son, was one of them.

"Do you think he has anything to do with this?" she said.

"I doubt it. He hasn't been around here in months. And I don't think he's really at the international criminal level."

Livy laughed. "You're probably right." He seemed gloomy still, distracted. "Hey, I bet Carine misses you," she said, grinning. Carine was a freshman whose sister knew Nelson's sister. For several months she had been remote in person and very warm online. Livy and Nelson would sit together in his room drinking flat orange soda, playing a tedious game of Risk, and the computer would plink, plink, plink with her messages.

"Oh, desperately," he said. He almost smiled.

"She's cute," Livy said.

He sat back, let go of his knees. "Yeah, she's cute." He sounded indifferent.

"What, you're too good for Carine Bronson?"

"She's fourteen. You want me to go out with her?"

"No, I don't know." She was talking just to talk, she realized. A bad habit. And a flirtatious gloss had crept into her voice, which happened sometimes when she was trying to cheer him up. "Do you think everybody's talking about us?" she said. As she said it, she realized that she hoped they were. "Do you think Elena is wondering what's happening—here?" She waved her hand, taking in the valley.

"Yeah, probably," he said. Elena was a girl at school who seemed to find Livy and Nelson amusing. Her other friends were a group of Honor Society girls who met at diners to discuss the shifting hierarchies of their grade, and she invited Livy and Nelson along sometimes to be educated. She could be quick and funny, and she could be mean. She had asked Nelson once if he could get her ecstasy, which he could not, and later she had denied ever having the conversation so vehemently that it had almost ended their friendship. She and her friends operated according to a complicated system of badness and goodness. "This is all probably super exciting to her," he muttered.

"Oh, come on. I bet she's worried."

"She can be both."

They sat quietly against the tree for a while. Livy grew restless. "Let's walk," she said. She got to her feet and tugged on Nelson's hands.

They picked their way down the hill and walked back and forth, up and down Prospect, from the store to the overpass just before Somersburg Road, Livy carrying her shoes. They decided to find some pot. Their nerves were jangled, although neither of them said so. Livy was beginning to feel odd pains in her body, in her shoulders and thighs, as if she had been holding an unnatural position for a long time. They went down to Brian Carroll's house, where the motorbike was still disassembled in the yard, and persuaded him to sell them a joint from his personal supply. He haggled with them over it, holding it between two fingers and peering at it as if appraising a piece of jewelry. He named a price and Livy and Nelson exploded with incredulity.

"*Maybe* half that," Livy said.

"I've smoked your weed before," Nelson said. "It's not that good."

"I got the market cornered right now," Brian said. "Where are you going to go?"

Livy rolled her eyes and dug some money out of her pocket.

"Profiteer," Nelson said.

From the Carroll backyard, Livy and Nelson picked their way along the creek bank to the bridge and smoked the joint in the deep shade of the high arch, looking out at the shallow water and the hill rising above it. "This tastes weird," Livy said.

"His stuff is terrible." Nelson stretched his legs out and leaned back against the stones of the bridge. They sat for a few minutes without talking. A siren started up, an ordinary ambulance in the distance, and just then Livy began to feel an invisible shift. It was all around her, like a vapor, in the shadowed space under the bridge and the sunny space over the water beyond it. She held very still. The air seemed to have darkened subtly.

"I'm feeling anxious," she said. She had always been good at identifying her emotions by their names, even when in the grip of them. She thought this was probably a talent, though not a great one. She looked up at the stone arch above their heads. "This bridge must weigh hundreds of tons. Thousands of tons."

"Hundreds, I think," Nelson said.

"I don't want to sit under it."

They crossed the creek and sat in a stand of syca-mores on the opposite side. Nelson patted her arm and her hair. "You're all right," he said.

"I'm all right." She ran her fingers across the under-side of his upper arm where the skin was soft and cool over the muscle. "You don't mind if I do this, do you?"

"It's nice," he said. He was looking up at the bright clouds as he said it, and keeping his arm very still;

keeping all of himself very still. It was nice. There was a cool buzz in the tips of her fingers.

She stared across the creek at the backyards of the houses between the bridge and the Lomath Sportsmen's Club which were separated from each other with chain-link fences but open to the water. "I love that gazing ball," she said. There was a violet glass sphere the size of a bowling ball on a white pedestal in Lena Spellar's backyard. "I hate it when I get like this," she added, her eyebrows and the corners of her mouth coming down.

"It happens to everybody."

"Not you," she said. He squinted at her sideways. She tipped her head back so the sun shone full on her face, which seemed to help. "You're like a stone," she said. He looked away. "A stoned stone. You are."

He laughed. She let her head drop back, felt its weight.

"Let's go up on the road," she said. "It's sunnier."

This was a mistake. When they came up over the embankment there was an argument going on at the end of the bridge. Lena and Dominic were talking to two policemen. Lena looked smaller to Livy than she ever had. Her blonde hair shone greenish in the sun, and she seemed to come no higher than the policemen's shoulders. Her hands waved in the air; she held something white in one small fist.

"It's empty," Lena said. The white object was an inhaler.

"We see it," said one of the policemen. "This area has still not been cleared."

"It's empty and I am out of refills."

Noreen was sitting up in her folding chair at the top of the steps, watching.

"There is a federal investigation going on here and nobody is passing through this perimeter at this time."

"I'll show you my prescription. I'll show you my inhalers." Lena's face was red and her eyes were wide with frustration.

Ron Cash was pacing at the edge of the conversation. "People need things," he said.

"I would suggest you all be a little more cooperative," the other officer said suddenly. "Maybe this would go quicker. Have you thought about that?"

"Who's not being cooperative?" Ron shouted.

"Be *quiet*, Ron, why do you have to be in this?" said Lena.

"You've been going through everything we have," Ron said. "We let you walk into our homes. Who's not being cooperative?"

"I can get my doctor on the phone for you," Lena said. "I have asthma attacks from allergies, from stress. I could have one any time. These are empty."

"I have medications myself," Noreen called. "Quite a few."

"You all have a choice about how long this takes," the second cop said.

"Are you trying to *kill* us?" Lena said.

"Put your hands down," said the first cop. "Get your hands under control. And your tone."

Lena took a step back, tears running down her face, and murmured something to Dominic, who was standing very still just behind her. Livy had once seen Dominic in a fight at school that had achieved iconic status afterward, with students who hadn't been there claiming that they had. It was just after the last bell, when people were milling in the front hallways and pushing for their buses, and Livy had stepped out onto the sidewalk and seen Dominic standing coatless under a cold January sky, with a friend attempting to hold him back, a shrimpish lackey of the type that seemed to swarm symbiotically around his large body. The other half of the fight was a tall, thin boy with a painfully acne-scarred face and long hair, the kind of kid who seemed to belong to no grade and no class, a phantasmic entity who might turn up anywhere at any time and who constantly projected a desire to be provoked into violence. He was screaming curses and threats, and they were collapsing the longer he went on and the more excited he got, so that "I'm going to fuck you up, motherfucker," finally became only "I'm going to fuck you, fuck you, fuck you," until Dominic stepped forward and hit him once in the jaw, knocking him down. Dominic didn't look angry, or even annoyed, at any moment during the incident. While the kid sat on the sidewalk, holding his face, Dominic turned and picked up his coat from where he'd dropped it and walked away to find his bus. Livy scanned Dominic now, knowing that his lack of expression did not mean that he wasn't about to do something violent. She wondered if the police could sense this also; she glanced at them and saw that they could.

"This is kidnapping," Lena said. "You can't do this to us, this is against the law, you can't just do whatever you want."

"She needs half an hour to go to the pharmacy," Noreen said.

Livy was gripping Nelson's arm. It seemed out of the question to turn and walk away; it would make them conspicuous.

"We'll get somebody down here soon," said the policeman in front, who was bald and looked tired. "We'll get some supplies to you. But we can't let people out."

"When? When will you get somebody down here?" Lena said. "There are diabetics. People have jobs, I have a job, people depend on me, I can't even use a telephone!"

She stepped toward him as she said this, her hands making arcs in the air, and for a moment the wild way she was moving made Livy think she might hit him. The policeman blanched and pushed her. It was a quick, practiced shove against her chest with his forearm, and she stumbled back into her son. Before she could straighten up or Dominic could begin to move, the younger policeman jumped forward and pressed a club against Dominic's chest.

"Don't," said the younger policeman. "You don't want to move."

Dominic's face was still blank, free of expression.

"Get back," the younger policeman said. His face was red. He stepped back, pushing Dominic at the same time so they fell away from each other like the halves of a split log. "Get *back*!" he said, and they did, Lena and Dominic and Livy and Nelson too, retreating back across the bridge while the police watched them.

Lena stopped as soon as they were out of sight and pressed both palms flat against her face. Dominic stood staring at her. "Fuck," he said. His mother bent her knees slightly, hid her face. "Fuck, stop crying, you're going to have an attack," he said. "*Stop*, Mom, please, come on."

Lena's face was mottled yellow and red. She turned away from them, waving her hands, and walked down the short slope to her own gate. Her hair was falling out of its elastic. She negotiated her front door and disappeared inside. Livy was shaken. She stared at Dominic, and he stared back.

"We'll get her refills," Dominic said.

"How?" Nelson said.

"Walk the fuck out and get them," Dominic said. He pointed toward the bridge.

Livy wondered how that could be done, what route to take. Her mind was racing. The part of her that had been surprised at the altercation was crumbling already, and she was moving something new into the gap it left. It didn't occur to her until much later that Dominic had said *we* and she had accepted it, just like that.

✳

It had been another difficult day for Revaz. He had put the battery back in the cell phone for a few minutes that morning, hoping for a message from the cousin. There was nothing. A slow-burn panic set in, which made him do stupid things like wave the phone through the air in search of a better signal, as if the nonexistent message were a butterfly he was trying to catch with a net. He was abandoned—the hustler cousin had taken his money and disappeared—or the phone signals were being interrupted, a thought that struck him as paranoid despite how appropriate paranoia was in his life now. Or the message he sent had somehow not gone through, or he had the wrong number. He approached the rendezvous

point again, but again could not get close. He filled the
water bottle in the creek. He crept back to the deer blind.
He had no idea what to do, except wait and repeat the
whole thing the next morning.

Revaz wanted a bottle of vodka, though it occurred
to him that if he had one he would almost certainly drink all of it, and that it would probably kill him.
This made him waver about wanting a bottle of vodka,
though it was still very tempting. Anger animated him
briefly as he went over a well-worn track of curses and
deprecations aimed at a few unspeakable bastards who
had done him serious wrong. He had trusted them. He
had trusted them insofar as anybody trusts anybody pro-
fessionally. But also, he had tried to make a little money.
This track always ended in self-loathing.

He ruminated on the mysteries of biology for a while
in the tree. He had not gone this long without a drink,
he reflected, since childhood. How strange it was to be
despairing because his life might be snatched from him,
and also despairing because the life he stood to lose was
so paltry. His will to live—was it the same as hunger?—
was insistent.

He couldn't stay in the deer blind any longer. If he
didn't eat soon he would be too weak to get away when
the time came. Once it was dark he climbed down in
search of food, walking almost blindly through the

woods with his hands up, trying to keep stray branches from hitting him in the face. His knee hurt terribly from lying on his back all day; it needed regular movement or it seized up. He had few ideas for finding something to eat. He would have to go down across the creek and try the garden in the yard of the white house.

He edged down through the woods to the road, crossed it in a few long strides, and slid down the bank into the creek. He got soaked to the knees in the crossing. On the far bank he walked straight through a patch of nettles in the dark, which brought tears to his eyes from pain and surprise. He thought at first he was having some kind of neurological event, the way his skin turned cold and then began to burn, but then he caught the smell of crushed vegetation and understood.

At the top of the bank he crouched for several minutes, panting, in a clump of weeds, gathering his nerve. Here the moon threw enough light that he could see. The garden was surrounded by a fence, but it was only chest-high. He trotted to the corner where the tomatoes were staked and pulled three fat ones loose, then dropped to his knees and ate them in under a minute. He hadn't intended to do this, prolonging his exposure in the yard, but he couldn't help it. Seeds and pulp were all over his face and shirt, and juice dripped down his wrists and into his filthy unbuttoned cuffs. He took two more tomatoes, then walked around through the gate and wrested loose a whole cabbage. He nearly fell in his hurry to get back across the creek.

Back in the deer blind, peeling the cabbage leaves loose and shaking the worms off, he felt a surge of joy. A little raw cabbage in his belly after several days without. This time he paused to smell the tomatoes for an instant before he ate them.

2

Livy was always the last person awake in the house. Her parents had been out most of the afternoon, sitting around Clarence Green's radio, and had gone to bed early. Livy sat in the kitchen, over the remains of a dinner of potatoes and beans, reading an adventure novel for children by the light of a citronella candle. It was a book she'd read many times when she was little, and it had a pleasant anesthetic effect on her brain. She had told her parents about Lena and the policemen on the bridge; they had told her to stay away from the roadblocks. She was becoming more and more tense as she waited for the boys to come collect her for the trip to the pharmacy. She hoped they might change their minds. She was afraid to go but couldn't say so without losing face. When Nelson tapped on the door she jumped and gasped so hard the candle almost went out. "Come in," she said.

Brian Carroll appeared behind him in the doorway, followed by Dominic, who pulled the door very quietly shut. "How are you doing?" Brian said. He was being polite. He was like that sometimes when he was planning or hiding something, lowering his head when he talked, retreating slightly into his oversized clothes. She'd once come across him nodding and apologizing manically to a school security guard who was scolding him for standing in a flower bed by one of the back entrances, a lit cigarette smoldering unnoticed at his feet.

"I'm okay," she said. The three of them came as far as the stove and then stopped and looked at her. They seemed apprehensive, bunching together in the middle of the room as if they had been wandering in the desert and she was their reintroduction to civilization. "You can sit down," she said. She moved the smoking candle to the middle of the table. They were out of tapers. Nelson was not a natural companion for Brian and Dominic; he was too quiet, and they were too tough. But they offered each other a kind of mutual amnesty based partly on being neighbors and partly on their shared interest in marijuana. Livy guessed she'd be regarded the same way if she were a boy, but being a girl she was naturally considered more suspect, more domesticated.

Dominic settled his bulk in a kitchen chair, which squeaked faintly. "We're going to walk down the creek," he said. "Nelson said you got past the cops on Somersburg doing that."

"Yeah, but it'll be harder going that direction," Livy said. "There are more police on Prospect than on Somersburg." Maybe she could pretend to have a stomachache and stay behind? But no, they wouldn't believe her, they would know she was afraid. And if they were going to be heroic, if they were going to go on a righteous mission to buy inhaler refills and rescue Lena Spellar, she would not want to miss it. Opportunities for heroism were rare in her life.

"Yeah, but the creek is farther from the road there, too," Dominic said.

"The cops did say they would send something," Livy murmured.

"Bullshit," Dominic said.

Livy thought he might elaborate, but he did not. "So, the Quick Drug," she said.

"Unless you have a better idea."

The Quick Drug was open twenty-four hours, and it wasn't far, less than a mile from the bridge, just past the point where Route 72 became First Avenue in Maronne. She looked at them from the doorway. The cat cried at her feet. "What if there are cops in the woods too?" Livy said.

"The whole Maronne PD is like fifteen people," Brian said. "They're not going to be everywhere."

"But they have the FBI too," Livy said.

"You think some FBI guy is sitting on his ass in the woods, waiting for us?" Brian said.

"I'm going to smoke a cigarette," Dominic said. He was tense. His stillness, when he paused by the door to let her step out of the way, appeared to be the product of huge, perfectly opposed forces. He closed the door behind him and then they heard the scrape of his lighter around the side of the house.

"I'm going to use your bathroom," Brian said, and withdrew.

Livy looked at Nelson. "What if the cops do stop us?" she said. Her stomach was starting to knot up. "Can they arrest us? Or do they just send us home?"

"I don't know," Nelson said. He paused, carefully unfolding and refolding a piece of tinfoil he'd found on the table. "Dominic said they wouldn't have a charge."

"He has a lot of experience with this?"

Nelson laughed. "He gives that impression." He looked at her. "I don't think you should come."

Livy was taken aback. "Why not?" Briefly and irrationally, she had the feeling of being uninvited from a party.

"Because I think the whole thing is probably a bad idea, kind of," Nelson said.

"But you're going."

"Yeah, but—" He waved his hands in frustration. "I don't want anything to happen to you."

"Well, likewise."

Brian came back from the bathroom, patting his freckled hands dry on the front of his shirt. Dominic had reappeared on the little square of bricks in front of the screen door. "We have to get some stuff before we go," he said. "So we'll meet up by the bridge in an hour, okay?"

"Okay," Livy said. Her insides were slicked with a kind of dread that was hard to distinguish from excitement. She was getting out, at least; out and away, through the woods. Her fingers and toes curled at the thought of it. Brian went out, closing the door quietly again, and he and Dominic disappeared into the dark. Livy got up from the table. "You want some coffee?" she said.

※

Livy and Nelson stopped at the end of the bridge and looked around. The moon had not risen yet, and it was still very dark. There was a faint suggestion of movement at the edge of the gravel lot below the church, and then a tiny light: Dominic smoking another cigarette. Brian was beside him, raising a pale hand in their direction. Livy and Nelson picked their way down to meet them.

"Do we have a plan?" Livy said. Nerves made her imperious.

"Let's get out of the parking lot first," Brian said, and Dominic dropped the end of his cigarette and stepped on it. They walked down under the bridge and stood on the gravel and dead leaves and fine sucking sand at the edge of the water. The arch was high and invisible over their heads, taunting them with the reflected sound of their nervous breathing.

"We'll walk down in the creek," Brian said. "And then, when we get to Maronne, we'll come up before the bridge and blend in."

"Blend in?" Livy said.

"It's two in the morning," Dominic said. "There's going to be nobody out."

"Okay, so nobody will see us," amended Brian.

"I'm saying if anybody does see us they're going to notice us. When's the last time you were in Maronne at two in the morning and didn't get picked up?"

"What do we do when we get to Quick Drug?" Nelson said.

"You have money?" Livy said.

"Yeah."

"Won't it look weird that we want this stuff in the middle of the night?" Livy said.

"No," Dominic said. "It's a twenty-four-hour drugstore. It wouldn't be open twenty-four hours if they didn't expect people to want prescriptions twenty-four hours."

"It'll take a long time," she said again.

"So we'll wait. Do you have a better idea?"

"No," Livy said. It was the second time he'd said that. He turned and walked away, and they followed him.

Not far from the bridge the undergrowth crowded them off the bank and into the water. It wasn't cold, but the creek bed was rocky and Livy knew it was full of rusty metal, bedsprings and bicycle parts and scrap steel that fell off the trains as they went around the turn. She had canvas sneakers on and plenty of things could go right through the soles. After a while she found herself in front; she was more knowledgeable of the underwater geography than the others were, and she moved faster than they did. In this part of the creek even the deep parts came only to their thighs and the bottom was smoother, sandier, less treacherous. She pushed through the deep water, her arms pivoting gently.

The bridge disappeared from view as they rounded the curve and the trees gathered close to the bank. Here the hill was too steep to be useful for anything, so it was empty, and had always been empty—bare and wild, so close to people, for so long. At the top there was bedrock that pushed straight out of the earth. All the hills of the valley were crowned with jagged bedrock like that, though it was hidden under the softness of the trees in summer.

The valley was deep black where they were. It was a warm night and the crickets sang in the undergrowth close to the water. Past the bend, the creek was shallow, filled with silt islands where whipping brambles grew between the sycamores. Livy led them through the burbling shallow water between the west side of the creek and the nearest sandbars. She heard somebody swear just behind her, and then the sound of clumsy, dangerous splashing. She stopped and turned.

"Are you okay?" she heard Brian say.

"Fuck. I guess," Dominic said.

"You stepped on something?" Brian said.

"It's fine. Let's go."

Livy tried to concentrate on her own feet. Looking into the water gave her vertigo: it was perfectly black. A rock shifted under her sneaker and she stumbled and reached out for a tree standing close to the water. As she looked up, a van coasted around the turn of the hill from Maronne.

"Shit," she said. "Get down, get down, get *down*."

She dropped to her hands and knees in the water. Nelson crouched down beside her and past him the dark shapes of Dominic and Brian fell into line. She could make out shadows against the lights high above the creek. The sounds of voices, people getting out of the van, and then the crackle of radios drifted down to them and flashlights snapped on. Livy tried to make herself smaller, her knees pressing against the stones.

Flashlight beams sliced down through the slender trees clinging to the far bank, making arcs of incandescent green. Livy's lips touched the water. There was not a single sound from the others, and with her face nearly in the water she was blind to everything and she could have been alone. She breathed in and out, slowly, five times.

She made herself look. She could still make out the shapes of the people standing next to the van, but the lights were panning farther up now, closer to the railroad bridge at the edge of Maronne. She sat up a little. Something sharp dug into the palm of her left hand and she took her weight off it.

Branches were crackling on their side of the creek. Lights advanced through the trees from the railroad bridge.

"Get back," she whispered. She grabbed a handful of Nelson's shirt and stumbled over the gravel, away from the island and toward the bank.

"Livy, they're coming from that way!" he hissed.

She dropped down again where the water was calm and dragged Nelson down with her, and it was the spot she remembered, a swimming hole where the water cut deep into the soft earth along the bank and heavy roots skimmed the surface, and they could almost disappear. She crouched neck-deep in the water. Next to her Nelson had taken hold of a thick root that curved above the water as smooth as a bare arm, and he was pulling himself back out of sight, against the small feathering roots underwater and the things that lived in them. Dominic was half out of the water, hiding behind a tangle of blackberry vines. Livy tipped her head back and pushed herself lower. She was submerged except for her eyes and nose and mouth, and she was looking up into the overhanging branches of the old trees. Far out over the center of the creek there was a patch of orange-lit sky.

On the far side of the creek, red lights shone through the weeds along the road: the van was backing up, going on its way. Livy lifted her head clear of the water to listen, and heard footsteps behind her, on the path that followed the creek a few yards back in the woods. A flashlight beam cut across the leaves of the tree above them.

They could hear men close now, ten or fifteen feet away. They could hear the noises their clothes made: the fabric on arms and legs rubbing together, the cracking of sticks under their boots. Water was running into Livy's mouth and it took all her concentration not to choke and spit. Time seemed to split into two tracks, so that there was no time to move and yet infinite time to imagine the disaster that loomed in front of her. The police would mistake them for the fugitive and they would shoot. She would die. Hiding was the wrong choice: if they had stood where they were and shown their hands, they would have only been arrested.

The flashlights waved and then there was a male voice, a few words. A single phrase reached them intact—"pick up"—and there was a murmured response and then the voices and footsteps faded away. For a count of thirty or sixty or ninety Livy stayed where she was, unconvinced of their good luck. There was no sound but a breeze in the high leaves. She lifted her head out of the water and took in a long breath. Relief expanded through her, like a balloon filling. She felt loose and warm and untouchable. Nelson was holding her arm under the water but he was invisible to her, back under the hanging roots. She squeezed his fingers and looked around for the other boys, not yet rising to her feet.

Was the night getting brighter? She could see the shape of Brian's head in the water; she thought she could see his closed eyes. Her legs nearly drifted out from under her. She floated there with Nelson holding on to her arm.

It felt like they waited ten minutes to move after the men were gone. Brian was the first to stand up. Dominic staggered and whispered, "Fuck, my foot."

"Can you walk?" she said.

"Yes, I can fucking walk."

They moved faster now, and kept to deeper water. Their clothes weighed them down. In five minutes they were out of the darkness of the trees and into the open, breathing tightly. They could see the massive arches of the old stone railroad bridge standing against the orange fog that hung over Maronne. They were past the roadblock and they could hear the trucks on the highway and see the lights around their edges, a bulb at each right angle as they rattled by.

The railroad tracks that followed the course of the creek crossed overhead on an iron bridge, and after they had gotten out from under its shadow they found themselves between retaining walls. The creek bed was silty and if they paused their shoes got sucked down into it and they staggered pulling them free. They walked along the side closest to the road, reasoning that the angles of sight were in their favor there, and glad for the guidance the wall offered in the dark.

They reached the arches of the stone bridge that marked the edge of Maronne. On the north side there was only the bare hill, showing in its granite face the marks of the dynamite charges that had cleared the way for the highway. On the south side were the first blocks of Maronne row houses, the first gas station, the clusters of warehouses, and, a little to the west, the scrapyards where the railroad tracks ended. The four of them climbed up out of the water under the high black arch and stood panting in the dark. The intersection was just as it had ever been; a truck and three cars eased to a stop at a red light as they watched, obedient even at 2:00 AM, a turn signal flashing like a pulse. Crickets and katydids sang.

"Wait until they go," Brian said.

They stayed under the bridge. The light changed to green and the truck and the three cars dispersed, two left, two straight ahead. They watched the red brake lights trail away up the hill. Livy thought the hard part might be over now. They walked out into the light of the streetlamps.

Livy could see Dominic's face now and it was clear that he was in some pain. He was limping and frowning.

"We could look at that," she said. Her legs were shaking slightly but she felt strong. She knew it was only the adrenaline still working in her, but she felt like skipping.

"Don't be stupid," he said.

They crossed the intersection and started up Broad. There were too many of them, Livy realized. Four people on the empty street like that, all together, not talking, the tallest of them limping; they were conspicuous. Under the streetlights she saw how her white shirt was stuck to her bra and she pulled it away from her skin, feeling the new cold. Their shoes squeaked and wheezed comically. Dominic alone had managed to stay dry above the knees.

The Quick Drug sat spilling icy light across a parking lot. Livy quickened her pace when it came into view, feeling an odd pleasure at the thought of doing this ordinary thing, a shopping trip. She'd brought a ten-dollar bill and intended to buy some candy. She pushed through the jingling door just behind Nelson and paused by the newspaper rack at the door, looking around at the makeup displays and rows of hosiery.

Dominic skirted around the edge of the store, down the side aisle, and met them at the empty pharmacy counter. His mouth was open and he was breathing audibly; his forehead was creased.

"You all right?" Nelson said.

Dominic lifted his chin and leaned back a little, moving his shirt aside at the hip. They could see a bit of his pale stomach.

"What?" Livy said.

"Look," he said.

It took a moment for her to understand what she was looking at. The handle of a gun was sticking out of the waistband of his jeans. She was speechless. Dominic leaned past her and tapped the bell on the counter with the palm of his hand.

"What the fuck is that for?" Livy said. "You said you had money!"

"But I don't have the *prescriptions*," Dominic said. He smiled.

"No, no, no," she said. She felt a thrumming through the air; it was the blood rushing to her ears. She looked at Nelson and he was closer to her than she expected, an expression of astonishment on his face. Brian appeared around a rack of sugarless candies, looking tense but unsurprised.

"Dominic, this is not a good idea, all right?" Nelson said, stepping forward with his hands out. "You haven't started yet. You don't have to start."

They heard a door open, invisible behind a bank of shelves at the back of the pharmacy area, and a man shuffled out. Nelson froze, halfway through his plea.

"Can I help you?" said the pharmacist. He was not a man. He was a boy, her own age. He was wearing a lab coat, something plaid underneath. He had a lanyard around his neck with keys hanging on it: *Cowlton Panthers*. He lifted a pair of glasses and put them on. "Um," he said.

Livy could imagine how they looked. Dominic was staring meaninglessly at him, the gun hidden under the edge of the high counter, and the three others stood in a rigid half circle behind him, all of them skull-faced with fear.

"Put your hands up," Dominic said. He lifted the gun over the edge of the counter and pointed it at him.

The pharmacist stared. His mouth opened.

"Put your hands up," Brian reiterated.

The pharmacist put his hands up. "There's only thirty-five dollars in the register and I don't have the key to the safe," he said. It sounded like he'd said it before.

"Livy, get back there with him," Dominic said.

Livy stared at him and flexed her numb hands. She felt the idiocy of her expression. "What for?" she said.

"No," Nelson said. "No."

He grabbed at her wrist, trying to watch Dominic at the same time, and missed. Dominic looked at her as if he didn't recognize her. His blankness was frightening, and she could not stop looking at the gun. She backed away from him and tried to walk through the little white gate beside the computer, but it didn't move and she pitched forward over it, both hands slapping the counter. She reached down to unhook the latch and her face burned.

"Don't push any alarms," Dominic said.

"What?" said the pharmacist.

"Don't do any alarm things."

"Hi," Livy murmured to the pharmacist. "Sorry." Her arms hovered in the air in front of her chest, her wet shirt.

"I have a list," Dominic said. He stepped forward and dropped it on the counter in front of the pharmacist: a square of paper, folded many times so it was small and dense.

"Okay," the pharmacist said. "Okay. I'll get them."

"Watch for an alarm," Dominic said to Livy.

"Okay," she whispered.

"There's no alarm," the kid said. "Don't shoot me. I'm not doing anything." His eyes were big, his shoulders hunched. Livy reached past him, picked up the paper and unfolded it, and held it up before his eyes.

"Go get them," Dominic said.

The pharmacist took the paper out of her hands and started opening drawers.

"Give me a lot of all of it," Dominic said. "As much as you have."

"What are you doing?" Livy said. "You're getting pills?"

"I needed some things too," Dominic said.

The pharmacist dropped a bottle cap and it skittered away across the floor. He looked at Livy with anguish.

"It's okay," she said. She picked it up.

Nelson was standing just behind Dominic. His mouth was open, he was breathing hard but silently, and his eyes were fixed on Livy and the pharmacist. When she looked at him he closed his mouth.

"Are the generics okay?" the pharmacist said.

"What?" said Dominic.

The pharmacist held up the paper. "I said, are the generics okay? They're the same as the name-brand drugs but cheaper."

"What? I'm not paying for them."

"I know." The pharmacist looked at the paper and then helplessly at Dominic again. "So, the name-brand ones," he said.

"Give me whatever you have the most of! Give me everything!" He shook the gun. "Hurry up!"

The pharmacist turned back to the cabinets. Livy could hear him whispering numbers to himself. She watched him, as she had been told to do. There was nothing within reach but shelves and bags of pills. There were no alarms. The pharmacist was counting, rolling pills off his fingers one by one, then tapping a box of inhalers down off a high shelf.

Nelson was at the front of the store. "There's a car in the parking lot," he yelled.

"*Fuck*," Brian said. "Fuck, fuck, *fuck*."

"We have to take him with us," Dominic said.

"What?" Livy said.

"We have to take him with us." He pressed close to the counter. The pharmacist stepped back, colliding with the shelves behind him. "If they want him they can fucking come and get him. Do you hear me?" he said to the pharmacist. "Maybe they can come pick you up and while they're there they can explain to us *what the fuck is going on!*"

The bells rang in front.

"Out the back," Brian said. "Now, go, *go.*"

Dominic limped around the counter and grabbed the pharmacist by the arm. He pushed him toward the door in the back wall. There was blood on the floor from his foot, long streaks of it on the tile. Far off at the front of the store a man called out, "Hello?"

They crashed through the bright air-conditioned cold of the storeroom, knocked the back door open, and ran as fast as they could through the parking lot, Dominic staggering on his bad foot with one hand gripping the pharmacist's arm. Livy had the bag of pills and inhalers knotted up in her fist to keep them from rattling. Nelson was next to her, looking back.

There was nobody watching. They dove across the intersection. Livy had never run like this. Her body burned. She followed the bobbing white of the pharmacist's lab coat, down the bank, across the tracks, dropping off the edge of the retaining wall into the creek and remembering just in time to hold the bag of medications up out of the water.

There was no thought of noise this time. They were all running as fast as they could and that imperative obliterated everything else. They splashed and fell, jumped up, battered their feet. Dominic must have been numb with adrenaline: he led them all, dragging the pharmacist by the arm. They passed the point where the roadblock stood on Prospect. They cut through the islands, through whipping brambles, and Livy's lip bled, her arms and legs stung with tiny scratches. They ran past the backyards, crossed the floodplain with what felt like marvelous ease after the rocky creek bed, and looped up under the bridge, into the intersection by the corner store.

They stopped there. Dominic took his hand off the pharmacist's arm. They straggled together; none of them could speak. They looked back over the bridge, into the dark. They had run a mile through the water, over the stones.

There were no lights. There was nobody coming.

"Oh, Jesus," Livy said. She sat down on the asphalt and held her head. The pharmacist sat down heavily beside her. "What the fuck did you do that for, Dominic?"

"What are we going to do?" Brian said. He was hunched over his heaving stomach, his freckled elbows sticking out like rafters. "What are we going to do? Dom?"

Dominic was walking in a little circle, long arms hanging, long fingers curled.

"They could be coming," Brian said. "Dom?"

Dominic fished in his pockets, looking up at the sky.

"You have to take him back," Livy said.

"I'll take him to my house," Dominic said. He turned around to look at them, the four of them sitting on the pavement.

"To your *house*?" Livy said, incredulous. "What are you going to tell your mom?"

"I'm going to tell her I got her refills and here's a pharmacist, and I'm sorry."

Livy stared at him. For a minute the only noise was their breathing. Then Brian straightened up. "What did they say?" he said.

Livy looked up at him. He was staring at the kid in the lab coat.

"What'd who say?" the kid said.

"The cops," Brian said. "When they blocked the road, what did they say?"

The pharmacist glanced back and forth between them. Dominic was still standing apart, looking up at the dark hill, as if this had all suddenly ceased to interest him.

"That they were looking for somebody, I don't know," the pharmacist said.

"You don't know? What, you weren't paying attention? Where do you live?"

The pharmacist blinked. "Riverview."

"Where the fuck is that?" Brian said.

"Stop yelling at him," Livy said.

Dominic turned toward them again, squinting, as if observing from a comfortable distance. "That trailer park on 72."

The pharmacist laid his head on his knees and stared in the direction of Sportsmen's Club. "Leave him alone," Livy said again.

"What's your name?" Nelson said.

The pharmacist didn't respond. Nelson leaned down toward him. It occurred to Livy for the first time that Nelson's buzzed head made him look slightly dangerous, even when he was speaking softly. "What's your name?" Nelson said again, and Livy had an ugly thought: Had he known about the gun? She watched him, still breathing hard, wondering. Everything was so opaque to her.

"Mark," said the pharmacist.

"Okay. Mark." Nelson patted the boy's shoulder.

"Let's go to my house," Dominic said.

Nelson offered Mark a hand, which he accepted. Brian kept spinning in place, shifting his weight from foot to foot, tapping his closed fist against his mouth. Mark was unsteady on his feet and Livy saw a slash of mud across his white coat.

"You messed up your coat," she said, but no one heard her. She paused in the road, arms crossed, refusing to follow them. She hated Dominic just then, and wanted to make a point of it. But no one noticed except Nelson, who looked back at her anxiously. She relented and caught up with them at Dominic's gate.

Dominic took great pains with the hinges on the screen door, and no one moved inside. Lena Spellar appeared to be a sound sleeper. Dominic led them into the kitchen, dropped into the closest chair, and retrieved a joint from a bag in his pocket. He pushed his shoe off with his good foot, wincing, and held a penlight close to the injury.

"Fuck," Brian said.

The sole was red, black, crusted. It had cracked open again when Dominic had taken off the sock and it was bleeding on the cushion. Brian picked a newspaper up off the floor and slid it underneath Dominic's foot and blood soaked the dirty pages.

"Mark, do you know what to do with this?" Dominic said.

Mark blinked at him. "I'm not a doctor," he said.

"You're not a doctor? I got confused and thought you were a doctor, Mark, what with the fucking coat and all."

"I'm a trainee tech. I'm only eighteen. I'm not even supposed to be there by myself, but the night guy called out, he has kidney stones . . ."

"Do you have any iodine?" Nelson said, but now all Dominic would say was "Shit," over and over.

Nelson found a bottle of Betadine in the bathroom upstairs and cleaned the cut. Blood had made a scrimshaw of the babyish wrinkles on the sole of Dominic's foot. The cut was three inches long, clean, slightly curved. Dawn was breaking and a kind of gray static filled the room. The sharp smell of marijuana hung over them; Dominic had lit the joint and was passing it back and forth with Brian and Mark, who looked grateful.

"What are you going to do with him, Dom?" Livy said. She pointed at Mark.

"Are you tired, Mark?" Dominic said. "You can have the couch."

Mark took a long drag on the joint.

"What are you talking about, he can have the couch?" Livy said. "What about your mom?"

Dominic looked at her, and then at Mark. "I guess he has to stay in my room," he conceded.

"Jesus Christ!" Livy said. She threw her hands in the air, appealing to him and to Nelson, who was standing there with the bottle of Betadine and an unreadable expression. "How are you going to keep people from finding out? Your *mom* for instance, who *lives in this house?*"

"Mark, you have to stay in Dominic's room and not make a fucking sound," Brian said. "Seriously, Dom, can you make him do that?"

Mark glanced back and forth between them, waiting for the resolution of this question as if it were not about him. There was something trusting about him, like a child in the back seat of a car.

"What if you say he's a friend of yours?" Nelson said. "Like, he's visiting?"

"How could he be visiting with the roads cut off?" Brian snapped.

"You know what? It's your problem," Livy said. "You were the one with the gun. I have to be home before my parents wake up." She glanced at Nelson, but he was not looking at her. His perpetual calm suddenly seemed suspicious. She made her way out through the living room, clumsy in her agitation. She tripped twice in the maze of furniture between the kitchen and the front door, and stopped on the front steps to pull herself together. The spring door squealed and Nelson was there, stumbling and blinking, as if the house had spat him out into the morning with her.

"Did you know he had that gun?" Livy said. "Were you all planning that before you came over to my house?"

"No!" He seemed shocked that she would think it.

She crossed her arms. Every muscle in her body felt like a closed fist.

"You don't believe me?" he said. "This is a nightmare. I shouldn't have done this, we should never have gone with them. I would never have gone with them if I had known—you don't really think I would do something like this on purpose?" He looked helpless, out of breath.

She hugged him quickly, squeezing his shoulder. "I believe you, I'm sorry," she said. "They'll let him go today, probably, when they get bored."

He took a deep breath and let go of her. How quickly he could regain control of himself, leaving only a puff of embarrassment in the air. "I have to get home before my mom wakes up," he said, his gaze leapfrogging away over her head. "Come up when you can, okay?"

"Okay."

After he was gone she stood for another minute at the Spellar gate, taking slow, deep breaths. It would be a hot, bright day. She could tell already by the blueness of the air, the way the noise of the insects carried. They were coming to the time of year when the crickets, desperate and close to the end, kept calling all day long from the ragged grass at the edges of mowed yards.

In the new light she could see what had happened to her arms when she ran through the brush on the silt islands in the creek. Her anger at Dominic was wavering, crackling like one radio station interfering with another: self-pity was coming through now, and dread. She was speckled and slashed with dried blood. Her jeans were clotted with burrs and she could feel her lip swelling. She hoped her parents might still be asleep. She was so tired she could hardly feel her feet.

The house was quiet. She crept up the stairs to her room and was asleep in minutes.

In less than an hour, there was rattling in the kitchen. She woke up slowly. Her muscles ached; she was lying on her stomach, her hands knotted together beneath her chest. A bird twittered insanely in the scrubby tree outside her window.

She took a shower, thankful that their water heater ran on gas, and found some clean clothes in the mess on the floor. She went downstairs, where her father was frying potatoes and making coffee. He had been digging the potatoes up out of the garden for weeks and the basement was filling with them. Normally he would be playing the radio at low volume, listening to the news. The silence felt strange, the room tight with omission. He looked up when she came into the kitchen.

"You're up early," he said. He peered at her. "What's wrong with your face?"

She remembered her cut lip. "I fell off my bike last night," she said. "Flipped over in the gravel." She showed him the scratches on her arms.

"You were riding your bike? In the dark?"

"I couldn't sleep."

"I hope you stayed away from the roadblocks."

"I did. I was just in the parking lot of the restaurant."

"Why would you do that? Ride your bike in the dark, with cops everywhere? I don't know what's wrong with you lately."

Livy was neither allowed nor forbidden to go out alone in the middle of the night. Her parents did not generally make rules. They just became annoyed when she did certain things.

"I'm sorry," she said. She couldn't meet his eyes and she guessed that she looked only sullen, not sorry at all. "I won't do it again," she offered. "The bike thing."

"This is a hard time," her father said. "Don't make it harder."

She went back to her room and lay in bed, wide awake, too tense to read or sleep. She imagined Dominic and Mark asleep in Dominic's room with Lena Spellar oblivious in the kitchen below them. *We are in so much trouble*, she thought, *so so so much trouble*, although the word seemed inadequate for what had happened. Her heart was racing. She pressed her hand across her breastbone.

When Livy was in ninth grade her health teacher had gotten frustrated with the class's lack of attention and had made them all sit on the floor beside their desks with their eyes closed for a meditation exercise, hectoring them to focus on calming their energy. Livy had found to her surprise that it worked, at least partially. If she closed her eyes her mind wandered irretrievably, so she'd kept them open and fixed on a cracked tile near her feet. Several minutes of focus had revealed profundities in the tile, in her shoelaces, in the underside of her desk—dirt and light, an alert calm. She'd practiced later in her room. She was fourteen then, unhappy at school, and the lonely summer that followed (Nelson was away with his grandparents in New Jersey) inclined her to a foggy mysticism. During solitary evenings in her room, the plaster walls seemed to bulge with unexpressed truths. She checked some books on meditation out of the library and put some candles on her dresser. She felt she was on the verge of a great discovery. But in the fall Nelson came back and school improved, and in the face of these banal comforts the spiritual urgency she had felt began to fade. She still lit her candles before bed and meditated briefly, but she was doing it in a perfunctory, corrective way, and she no longer felt she was on a path from one place to another. She never told Nelson or anyone else about meditating. But she still found that it could work, from time to time.

She stared at the lamp that hung from her bedroom ceiling and began to feel a pleasant heaviness in her face; she even slept for a little while.

At ten she roused herself and found the house empty. She went out to the yard to see what her parents were doing. They were working on a cold frame in the garden and her mother was standing beside it, resting her back.

"Come here, Livy," she said. They were a pale family and they were all sunburned, which gave them the sad, doomed look of people outflanked by their climate. Her mother pulled at her sticky dress and brushed her hair out of her eyes. "So you were out last night," she said.

They stood looking at each other. Livy's father cursed softly inside the cold frame and knocked a jammed staple gun against a plank.

"Yeah," Livy said.

"Your dad thinks we haven't taught you any common sense."

"Does he?" Livy was unsure of the role she was supposed to play in this conversation. The truth of what had happened so dwarfed the offense they were scolding her for that it was hard to keep the right expression on her face—shame, a touch of defiance.

Her mother nodded. She kept nodding for a minute, looking at her feet, and then she sniffed and Livy saw that she was crying. Livy started as if someone had struck a match in her face. "I'm really sorry. Don't—"

"Don't do stupid things right now, all right?" her mother said. She wiped her eyes with dirty fingers and shook her head. Livy backed away, dismissed. Halfway to the house she turned and looked back at the garden: her father and mother were both in the cold frame now, pacing with a measuring tape, as if on an ordinary day.

※

Livy knocked on Dominic's door at eleven, when it was reasonable to visit, and caught her breath when Lena answered. "Livy?" she said.

"Is Dominic here?" Livy said.

Lena looked surprised. Livy was a bookish girl, an honor student. She had never visited Dominic before. "In his room."

"Upstairs?"

"Yeah. Top of the stairs, in the back."

Livy grinned nervously and stepped through the doorway, past the scent of Lena's jasmine perfume. "Thanks," she said.

The bedroom door was closed, and Livy knocked several times before Dominic came and opened it. He looked a little surprised to see her. "I thought you were pissed at me," he said.

"I am. You're an asshole."

He laughed. There was something genteel about it, his lack of concern. "What are you here for, then?"

"To keep an eye on things, I guess."

He stepped out of the way. The window opened onto the porch roof at the back of the house, and Mark was out there, peering around the curtain at her.

"He's outside?" she said.

"It's all right," Dominic said. "Nobody'll see him."

Mark said, "I'd come in, but—" He held up a lit cigarette. His expression was blank, or simply earnest; she couldn't tell. In daylight he was solid and pale, like a piece of carved soap. She thought she recognized his type: boys who were punished often in school but didn't seem to notice, as if life were naturally a string of humiliations.

"I'll come out," she said. She crawled out the window, scraping her scabbed elbow on the window frame. The asphalt shingles were hot. She crouched on her heels. Dominic climbed through the window with a practiced, graceful movement, frowning in concentration, and then sat back to pick the bits of shingle off his palms. He favored his hurt foot.

"Does your mom know?" she said.

"She knows we went to the drugstore," Dominic said. "I gave her her refills."

"Does she know about him?" She pointed at Mark.

"She doesn't come in my room."

"I've been here before," Mark said suddenly. He was looking thoughtfully down at the creek, the trees on the far bank. "I didn't even know this place had a name. I drove through a couple of times when there was a detour on the highway after the flood."

Livy's split lip was starting to throb. "I'm sorry about this," she said. He didn't react. She looked at Dominic. "You should let him go, Dom."

Mark looked up as if she had said something impolite.

"The cops wouldn't let him through even if he got up there," Dominic said, pointing up at the bridge, meaning the barricade beyond it. "You know that, right, Mark? You're stuck down here as long as we are."

"The longer you keep him here, the more trouble we're in," Livy said.

"We're already basically in jail," Dominic said.

She looked down over the edge of the porch roof at the hydrangea bush in the yard, the patio umbrella tipped over in the grass. "What about your parents, Mark?" she said.

He fixed his eyes on her and raised his eyebrows slightly. He seemed surprised by her interest. "We don't really—" he said. "We don't talk. I've been staying with my sister."

"So she's looking for you, probably, right?"

"I don't know. She doesn't really check up on me."

Livy was irritated. Irritation was an emotion so un-dersized for the occasion that she seized on it gladly. She was irritated with Mark for his passivity, for the lumpish way he sat on the asphalt, and for his evident failure to be as worried as she was, which made her look foolish.

"I don't want to go to jail," she said, her face tight.

"Why would you even fucking say that?" Dominic said. "Nobody wants to go to jail. You think other people go because they want to? Jesus."

Brian knocked on the window behind them. Livy jumped.

"I brought handcuffs," Brian said. He held up a pair and they dangled brightly against the dark interior of the house.

"What the fuck!" Dominic said. He grabbed at them excitedly. "Where did you get these?" Brian handed him a blunt little key, and he reached in Mark's direction. "Give me your wrists, Mark."

Mark looked back and forth between the two of them. The cigarette was still lit between his fingers. He held it up.

"Finish it and give me your wrists," Dominic said.

"Don't do that, that's shitty," Livy said. "He's not even trying to get away." She thought she saw fear in Mark's still face. His mouth was slightly open. He took another drag on the cigarette, flipped it over the edge of the roof, looked at the two boys again, and then held up the pale undersides of his wrists. Dominic snapped the cuffs shut.

They all looked at the handcuffs. Mark's nails were short and dirty. "They're too tight," he said finally. He had a very low voice.

"I can fix it," Dominic said. He fumbled over them with the key. "Shit, they're pinching." He worked in silence for a minute. "What about now?"

"That's fine," Mark murmured.

"Ha-*ha*," Dominic said, a triumphant exhalation. He leaned against the siding.

There was someone on the bridge, but Livy couldn't tell where the person was looking. "Look," she said, pointing.

Dominic squinted at the figure on the bridge. "They can't see us from there."

"Fine. Do what you want," Livy said. "I'm leaving."

She heard a dog barking as soon as she came out onto the front steps, and saw it a moment later, when she was closing the gate behind her. It was a big shepherd mix, standing in the intersection in front of the store, head and tail low, legs stiffly planted, and there were two men standing about fifteen feet in front of it, one of them holding a large cardboard box.

Livy crossed the road to get a better look and saw that the two men were police. *Oh Christ*, she thought. Jocelyn stood in the doorway of the store, biting her lip.

"Whose dog is this?" yelled one of the policemen.

The dog moved back a little and stopped. It was growling so loudly Livy could hear it from where she stood, thirty feet down the low road. One of the men made a move to set the box down and the growl collapsed into furious barking. Jocelyn removed the prop from her door, stepped back into the shadows, and let it swing gently, silently shut.

"Whose fucking dog is this!" yelled the policeman.

At the sound of his voice the dog bounded sideways and stopped, squaring up to them, and Livy saw a piece of chewed-off rope as long as her arm trailing from its collar. The dog was ecstatic with rage. It crouched, jerked forward, retreated, and then settled into its stiff-legged pose, the bunched fur on its spine vibrating slightly. Ron Cash was standing on the porch of the house that shared a wall with the store.

"Is this your dog?" yelled the cop.

"No-o," he said, letting the word waggle in the air mockingly.

"These are medical supplies," said the one holding the box. "You'd better figure out who this dog belongs to, you hear me?"

"That dog is *your* problem," Ron said, a little louder this time.

The first cop had taken his gun out of the holster. The second cop tried a second time to set the box down, and a second time the dog lunged forward and stopped. The door of the store opened and Paula stepped out. "Don't you shoot that dog," she said. "Don't you *dare* shoot that dog!"

"*Whose dog is it?*" cried the first cop again.

A door slammed. Livy jumped and looked over. She could see Jerry Olds come down the side steps from his house in his cautious way, as if his feet hurt, and walk across his steeply tilted yard. He stopped at the bare patch in the grass beside the doghouse and she saw him shake his head and walk on toward the dog, no faster than before. Jerry Olds rarely left his property. He was a silent, jagged presence, an unloved neighbor widely believed to be deficient—morally, perhaps mentally. Many years before he'd punched one of the neighbor boys, fourteen at the time, in the jaw, for reasons that were never clear: just came out of his house and hit him, and went back inside. No one had called the police about it.

"It's my dog," Jerry said when he reached the edge of the road.

"Get it the fuck out of here!" said the first cop. "These are medical supplies!"

"Why won't you just let us out so we can take care of our own business?" yelled Ron from the steps.

Jerry stood in the grass and whistled to the dog. The dog ignored him.

The cop waved his gun helplessly in the air. "I don't want to, but I will," he yelled.

"You're murderers!" said Ron. "He's a *pet*, he's a *domestic animal*!"

"I'm going to come out there," Jerry said. He edged into the intersection, eyes on the dog. "Come here, Chief, you piece of shit."

The dog heard him and turned. He appeared to be wracked with great waves of emotion. He barked again at the cops, hunched his shoulders, and began to whine softly. He looked at Jerry, and Livy saw the whites of the dog's eyes.

"That's it, you little bastard," Jerry said. He was smiling, which Livy had never seen him do before. The cops were wide-eyed. One still had his gun half-raised. The dog shivered and whined and Jerry held out his hand.

"There's a boy," he said. He closed his fingers around the collar.

There was a thump as the cardboard box hit the asphalt, and both cops turned and walked away, moving as fast as they could without running. The one with the gun looked over his shoulder several times. Livy's stomach turned. They had been scared and people had seen it, and they knew it. The cardboard box sat abandoned at the end of the bridge.

"I hope it's what they say it is," said Paula.

Ron was shaking his head vigorously, pivoting a little on his stiff leg. "Acting like the dog is the problem," he said. "The dog lives here. The dog is doing his job."

Jocelyn came out of the store. Livy stayed where she was, watching the bridge where the police had turned the corner and disappeared. Lena Spellar's house huddled in her peripheral vision, compact and yellow, a fan in an upstairs window turning slowly in a light wind. The cardboard box in the intersection seemed to be soaking all the pigment from the scene. Paula came down from the steps to retrieve it, and Livy followed her. She needed to know what was in it. If the box was full of medicine then the trip the night before had not been necessary and she and Nelson and Brian and Dominic had caused this trouble for no reason at all. She crept into the store after them, hoping that no one would pay her any attention.

Noreen was leaning on the counter, slightly out of breath. "It's just getting worse and worse out there," she said. "Shouting all the time. I don't even want to step out to see anymore."

Paula sat down in a folding chair and braced one arm across the counter like she was holding it in place, her large glasses sliding down her nose. Jocelyn crouched on the floor to cut open the tape on the top of the box.

"Livy, what are you doing out there?" Noreen said. "It's not safe for kids to be out now."

"I was just walking by," Livy said, her voice a whisper. To Noreen, she would always be eight years old. The scratches on her face and arms felt large and impossible to miss; she licked the scab on her lip. Noreen's eyes were hidden by the reflection on her thick glasses, and Livy fought the feeling that she was being examined.

"They brought insulin," Jocelyn said, lifting out plastic-wrapped packages.

"Oh, thank God," Noreen said. "I'm trying to keep mine cool in the basement, but it's hard."

"So they were paying attention when Lena was screaming at them," Paula said.

"She needed inhaler refills too," Livy said quietly, trying to see over Jocelyn's shoulder without moving from her place by the door.

"Are there any in there?" Paula said.

Jocelyn searched the bottom of the box. "No."

Livy let out a long breath, as quietly as she could.

"Maybe they'll come back with it," Noreen said.

Jocelyn sat down beside the box, cross-legged, like a child. "I don't like this," she said. Her voice was faint. "How long are they planning to leave us down here, if they're bringing us medicine? I want to see my *son*."

"I saw Tobias for a minute this morning," Paula said. "On White Horse Road. He says he doesn't think it'll be much longer. He's about to lose his mind over it." She tipped her head back suddenly and inhaled through her nose, and Livy saw that she was crying. She felt panicky: Paula with slick cheeks, pink eyes.

Ron Cash shoved the door open, making the bells jingle on their string. "We have to find this guy." He was sweating and his voice was more strained than usual, high-pitched and hoarse.

"He's not here," Paula said. "They've already looked through everybody's house."

"That's naive," Ron said. "That's really naive."

"Livy, are you all right?" Noreen said. "You look shook up. Have a soda or something."

"Thanks," Livy said. She went over to the silent refrigerator and took out a warm cream soda.

"This won't be over until they get him," Ron said. "You all are fooling yourselves if you think otherwise. If they leave without him, they lose, and they're not going to be the ones to lose. I guarantee you that."

"Knock it off," Noreen said.

"That's not just the state police out there. That's the FBI and the CIA, the ones in those black four-by-fours. It's on the radio. Tobias knows. She'll tell you." He pointed at Paula.

"I'm not going to help you panic people," she said.

Noreen ignored him. "Don't worry about the money," she said to Livy. "You're all red."

"Thanks," Livy said again, and excused herself to the road outside. Behind her she could hear Ron's cracked voice wending higher and higher.

✳

She found Nelson in his parents' garage. The door was open to the halfhearted parenthesis of the driveway, and he was dragging bags of potting soil from one wall to the other. She told him about the dog and the box of insulin. Nelson sat down on a child-sized decorative bench and listened to her with his spidery hand spread out across his forehead.

"Sounds like it could have been worse," he said when she was done. "I'm surprised Jerry came out to get the dog, like he gives a shit." Jerry generally gave the impression that he would not care if his own house were burning down.

"I know. I thought it was going to die." Tears welled up in her eyes at the thought, and she brushed them away. "I don't even like that fucking dog." She stood there rubbing her arm for a minute. "What are you doing out here, anyway?"

"My mom wants me to clean up."

She stared at him and at the garage: the workbench at the back, the particleboard hung with hooks, the corners crowded with shovels and rakes. "That's her priority?"

He picked up the bench he'd been sitting on. "I'm just moving things from one side to the other."

"This is already the cleanest garage I've ever seen," Livy said.

※

Livy's father came into the kitchen around six that evening, while Livy was peeling potatoes and her mother was attempting to make cornbread with powdered milk.

"I was just talking to Clarence," he said. He was out of breath in the doorway. He had taken his glasses off. "He told me about the Quick Drug."

Her mother stopped oiling a pan. "What?"

"Well, Livy?" her father said. He was holding his glasses in front of his chest, his thumb heedlessly on the lens.

"I'm sorry," Livy said. It was weak, she could hear how weak it was. She stood there gripping a cold potato.

"What are you talking about?" her mother said.

"They went to the Quick Drug," her father said.

"I'm sorry," Livy said again.

"That kind of—" Her father waved his hand, and it collided with the doorframe. "I wouldn't have— you startle a cop in the dark and you get *shot*, did you even—"

"You went past the police?" her mother said.

"We wanted to get prescriptions. Lena was out of inhaler refills."

"Why would you go along with that?" her father said. "You trying to impress some people? Dominic and Brian? You want to hang around with that kind of person? You want to look tough?"

"No." She looked at him: he must not have known about the robbery and Mark. He couldn't know, he wasn't horrified enough. Livy's mother was staring at her, open-mouthed.

"And Nelson too," her father went on. "I was really surprised. I thought he was at least smarter than that."

"You thought we wouldn't hear about this?" her mother said. "And you told us, what, you were riding your *bike*?"

Livy avoided their eyes. Her heart was pounding.

"That is not the way to handle things," her mother said. "It's not your job to fill Lena's prescriptions. This isn't like you."

That was true, Livy thought, it wasn't like her. She usually had sense. But maybe it was just that she had had so few chances to do stupid things before. Maybe she was actually a person who would do stupid things all the time, if it seemed likely that other people might see her doing them and think she was brave.

"Somebody could have gotten killed," her father said. "Do you understand that?"

"Yes." She tried to compose her face.

"You do?"

"Yes."

"You're not leaving this house again until this is over. Do you understand?"

She nodded. He turned and walked out.

He didn't come back for dinner. Livy and her mother ate in punitive silence and then retired to separate corners of the house, Livy to her room with a candle, her mother downstairs to the porch with a kerosene lamp. The darkness of the house was oppressive, the candle making little difference. Livy oscillated between a tired fatalism and total, shattering amazement at the scope of the disaster that she was in. As a child, she once spent a morning at school idly chewing on the end of her pencil and then became convinced that she had given herself lead poisoning. She didn't know that modern pencils were made of graphite, and she had only a vague idea of what lead poisoning would do to her. She sat on a bench in the library area and stared into her hands for an hour during the reading break in the afternoon, certain that a destructive force was irremediably nested within her guts. This was the template for every moment of dread she felt afterward. She could almost see Dominic's house from the skylight in her room. She could see the Sportsmen's Club, the outline of the folksy weathervane stuck absurdly on a fake cupola at one end of the quarter-acre sheet-metal roof. The Spellar house was next to it, in a row hidden from her by the trees crowding together over the Black Rock Creek. Mark's presence practically glowed from the midst of those trees. What a ridiculous idea to think you could hide anything, ever, from anyone.

Livy lay in bed, staring up at the sloping ceiling and the shadows the candle threw around the loose edges of the pictures she had taped there when she was fourteen—mostly landscapes cut from copies of *National Geographic* and photographs from a Time Life publication she'd found in the free bin at the library, teenage boys bare-knuckle boxing in a barn, young couples draped over each other with exhaustion at a Depression dance marathon, a row of masked girls grinning manically at a 1950s cotillion. She was easily taken in by the uncanniness of old photos, their vibrating stillness. She heard her father coming in, heard him make his way up the stairs from the basement to the kitchen and open a drawer in the sideboard. She didn't approach the edge of the loft to see what he was doing, because he would have heard her, but she could tell anyway: he had dug out the notebook where he kept track of the garden and was sitting in his designated chair at the kitchen table, working over his lists and diagrams and drinking a glass of wine. He had calmed down, then.

Livy slipped downstairs, past the kitchen, not turning to acknowledge her father from the doorway. They sometimes pretended to be less aware of each other than they were, to buttress the weak privacy of the house. From the ground floor she could see her mother through the front windows, sitting on the porch with the kerosene lamp, reading a book. Their house was full of books and her parents had read most of them so long ago that the books were new to them again. Livy stepped onto the porch and closed the door behind her.

"Do you have any magazines?" she said. She cleared her throat.

Her mother glanced up at her, lowering her book. It seemed to take her a moment to focus on Livy's face and understand her question. "There are a couple on the bedside table," she said.

Livy nodded and looked out into the yard. This was a new strategy: she would pretend that it was up to her to decide when the argument was over. This was generally her mother's prerogative—after a little while, a couple of hours or perhaps half a day if the offense was more serious, she would appear in Livy's room, speaking in a light, friendly tone but not making much eye contact. The weight of the problem would just fall away, leaving nothing behind. Livy stood there interlacing her fingers behind her back. "You mind if I take a couple to read?" she said.

"No, go ahead," her mother said. There was a long silence. "There are bats in the roof," she said finally. "I can hear them rustling around up there and squeaking."

Livy looked up at the rafters obediently. Her mother was a great changer of subjects.

"I don't know if I'm supposed to think they're a nuisance," her mother went on. "They eat the mosquitoes. But I think most people run them out."

"I like them," Livy said.

"Me too," her mother said. "Even if they do shit all over the place." She squeezed Livy's knee, and then gave it a pat.

✳

Another day with no text message from the cousin; another day unable to get close to the meeting place. The raw cabbage and tomatoes had gotten Revaz's bowels moving and he had had to dig a hole with a stick behind the blackberry bush. It was hard to dig with the stick, and he was sweating and slapping mosquitoes at the same time. It made him feel old and frail. After a while he dropped the stick and dug with his hands, the earth packing in under his fingernails.

If they arrested him and sent him back, he would die in prison. It would likely be tuberculosis that got him—it was everywhere in the prisons and the drugs did nothing—or a heart attack. He had high blood pressure and nobody got to see a doctor in prison unless they were already half-dead. He had visited many prisons and he knew.

He had written six stories about the prisons, and had even gotten an allowance to bring along a bloody-minded photographer who talked the men into pulling up their sleeves and showing their sores. The smell was asphyxiating everywhere: he'd seen twenty-two men in a single holding cell designed for six, and half the toilets had no water. The series had sold to a tabloid and he'd kept the gas on in his apartment for three months with the earnings, before the inevitable call came from some municipal undersecretary and the assignment was shut down.

He'd had a few brilliant ideas in his life and every one of them had started with money and ended with a beating. Inmates got no phone calls, were allowed no letters. Sometimes they went without personal visits for months or years—their request paperwork was lost, or they failed to keep up their end of the elaborate network of obligations that was the economy of prison life. A visiting journalist could carry messages to the men for money. Another journalist brought this fact to his attention, a colleague with a summer house in the mountains, and he was persuaded. He was still in debt from when his parents were dying. They had tried private care, not that it had helped. And he had other debts as well.

There was quite a bit of money at first. His colleague put him in touch with a man named Beridze, who met him in a café, wearing a shearling jacket and cheap shoes, and explained that he would act as a broker between Revaz and the many people who needed to communicate with prisoners, many of whom were Beridze's friends. He smiled when he said "friends," in case Revaz might fail to understand what he meant: he was *kanonieri qurdebi*, the mob. The *kanonieri qurdebi*, existing half in and half outside of prison as it did, had urgent communication needs. He and Revaz agreed on a rate of payment, and letters began arriving at Revaz's apartment, an outer envelope addressed to him and a smaller envelope inside, sometimes immaculate and sometimes folded and smudged, with the prison number and the recipient's name on it. Revaz could visit the prisons easily, even though his series had been discontinued. He still had his press pass, and the guards were indifferent to all matters outside of life and death and their own hustles. For a year he made regular visits.

His address was circulating, he realized uneasily in the winter of that year. More and more messages arrived. There were no return addresses, and the only direct contact he had was with Beridze, who dropped by his apartment once a month with a bottle of sherry to make sure he was still "comfortable." The money was wired into a second bank account that he set up.

If he'd been telling his sister Anna this, he would have said: *Those poor men. You can't imagine their isolation.* As the word got out he was sometimes approached directly by mothers and girlfriends who had heard he could get into the prisons, and for them he reduced the rate for his services. He saw real gratitude in their eyes. There was that, at least.

Of course, Anna was not an idiot. She would have said: *And the rest? Nothing but love letters, are they? Love letters from the* kanonieri qurdebi *to their many, many friends.*

The beating came in the spring. He was walking home from work and the gutters were trickling with melted snow. They came up behind him and pulled his jacket over his head, so he saw no faces. It was over very quickly. His nose was broken and two ribs were cracked.

He had laughed later, in his apartment, trying to think who might have done it. Because there were so many people he'd carried messages to by then, and in parsing out the matter he had to think not only of them and their friends and their many business connections—most of whom he could only guess at, because why would he ask?—but he also had to think of their rivals, and *their* business connections and friends and wives and mistresses, and this vast spreading growth of sympathy and antipathy was the actual fabric of society. He'd gotten into a bad place in it, and that was all he knew.

And one of the messages, maybe, had been about the ferry. At any rate, the police said it had been. He couldn't say; he never read them.

When it got dark he climbed out of the tree and walked in the woods. His stomach no longer hurt from hunger, but food was constantly on his mind. Potatoes: boiled mostly, with sour cream. Heavy, filling beer. The marrow from the neck bones in the soup pot, scraped out and eaten with salt.

Revaz knew he couldn't wait forever for a hustler who wasn't coming, living on stolen cabbages. But he was not brave enough for this game, really. If he wasn't careful he would simply sit in the tree until he starved or had a heart attack. It was a great mental effort to contemplate the brave and probably futile things he could do—the mad dash he could make over the hill, cars he could steal. Even if he got past the police, how would he find his way?

Had the people in the white house noticed the stump where he had pulled the cabbage loose? He had a sudden bolt of insight into fairy stories about imps who come in the night and steal little things, mangle chickens and break crockery. That was what he was now, a shadowy creature who picked at the edges of daytime lives.

※

Livy could not concentrate on the magazines, and as the night grew later and she felt no urge to sleep, her anxiety began to rise again. She straightened the books in the shelf above her bed; she'd read them all many times. Her parents had gone to bed. They would find out about the robbery eventually. There must have been cameras in the pharmacy. She kept picturing the two of them side by side in the kitchen with their hands pressed across their eyes; shock and bottomless disappointment. Her nearest cousin, a weedy boy in Creek County, had been brought home twice by the police, in the style of teenage boys: once for possession of drug paraphernalia—a glass pipe—and once for something she couldn't remember, some teenage crime extrapolated from insolence, from hanging around. She pondered the fact that what she had done was much worse than anything the cousin had ever done, despite his outsized reputation in the family. She stood in the middle of her room, shoulders hunched, flinching in the dead air.

It was hot but she didn't want to open the skylight because mosquitoes would come in. She paced. Sweat bloomed under her hair. She tried to write in her journal but got no further than *Still stuck here*. She thought about writing down what had happened at the pharmacy but dismissed the idea immediately on the grounds that the journal could be used as evidence against her in a criminal trial. She doubled back on this thought and examined it closely for signs of hysteria or exaggeration, and found to her dismay that it was sound. The room was stifling. She shuffled down the stairs.

She took a cigarette from her mother's pack, which was in the pocket of a raincoat hung by the door. She had smoked only two or three cigarettes before in her life, but this seemed like a good time for one. She found the matches in the cabinet over the stove and pushed the front door open as quietly as she could.

The night was brighter than she had expected. An oval moon hung over the hill across the creek. The yard spread out before her like a basin: the garden at the bottom with the garage and the massive privet bush beside it, the hills sloping up and away. She had sometimes slept in a tent in the yard when she was younger, giddy with the exposure of it, the animal secrets in the grass. She would wake up to find slugs in the shoes she'd left by the tent flap.

She walked out into the middle of the basin, wondering if going into the yard counted as leaving the house. She lit the cigarette, which made her cough. She felt a crinkle in her chest like a paper bag. Her mother smoked a strong brand. She walked deeper into the dark yard, inhaling lightly, cut grass sticking to her wet feet. There was a broad avenue of grass with trees on both sides leading to the driveway the Markos shared with the neighbors; she intended to go that way and walk the loop of the driveway down to the creek on the other side. But as she got closer to the woods she was afraid.

She stopped and regarded the trees. The feeling was clear and persistent, the voice of a matter-of-fact child saying *Don't go near the woods at night*, and Livy realized, standing by the garage on the tame, newly cut grass with the dark trees right ahead of her, that it was the voice of Little Red Riding Hood. She'd had a recording of the story when she was little and this was the actor's voice speaking from the center of her chest, giving her a piece of eternally solid advice. She took a small drag from the cigarette and stayed where she was. She was safe by the garage wall with the moon shining weakly down. There was a flash of white in the woods and the sound of dry branches breaking and undergrowth giving way—a deer leaping, escaping.

A man walked out of the woods. Livy's breathing hitched in her throat. She put her free hand on the planks of the garage wall behind her.

It was clear that he saw her. He took a few steps out of the underbrush at the edge of the woods, moving the vines of blackberries and multiflora roses delicately out of his way, and then stopped on the grass and brushed off the front of his pants. He put one hand in the air: a wave. Livy was suddenly inverted, her insides blank with shock, her consciousness straining outward. He had been there the whole time she walked in the yard, lit her cigarette, lingered by the garage; he had heard her coughing, had been watching while she scratched the mosquito bites on her legs. Her right hand scrabbled over the boards behind her and closed over the handle of a potato fork on a nail. It was a blunt-tined pitchfork with a short, worn handle, a garden tool that looked more dangerous than it was. She leveled it at him.

He did not move. They stared at each other. Livy shuffled sideways to the corner of the garage, holding the potato fork out in front of her. The house was behind her, a straight shot. She paused at the corner of the garage, breathing hard, and the man lowered his hand.

She ran. The potato fork swam along beside her with the pumping of her arm. She reached the porch and tried the door; it was locked. She had come out of the kitchen door, on the other side of the house, and her parents must have locked this one before they went to bed. Her stomach twisted. She hit the door twice with the flat of her hand and looked back. He was still standing at the edge of the trees, looking after her, but now his hands were hanging at his sides. He was making no move to follow her.

She shook the hair out of her eyes, wiped the sweat off her forehead. His shoulders were slumped, his body thick around the middle. He wasn't following her, but he wasn't retreating, either.

She recognized him. He was the man in the photo.

"*Shit*," she said, pronouncing it so forcefully that saliva dribbled over her lip. He was wearing a white shirt; she could see the gleam of eyeglasses. She looked down at her shaking hands, remembered the cigarette, and threw it away.

He disentangled himself from the edge of the woods. The white shirt shifted and sagged against the dark undergrowth, and then he was out in the moonlight, walking carefully across the grass with both hands held out in front of him, palms forward. The moon shone down on his small round head. He stopped by the arborvitae a few yards from the porch and raised his hands higher. "Please?" he said.

Livy could see the shape of the top of his head, his shoulders, his supplicating hands, but his face was dark; only the frames of his glasses stood out. To his eyes she was probably only a shadow at the edge of the porch. She was glad for that. She held the potato fork out farther, to make sure he saw it.

"Please?" he said. He walked down the slope toward her. His expression was anxious. He looked about fifty, in a button-down shirt with the sleeves rolled up and dark pants. There was a gleaming metal watchband on one upraised wrist. His hair stood up in tufts.

Livy's mouth was closed tightly and she was breathing very hard through her nose. He stopped a few feet away, below her on the grass.

"Please," he said.

His accent rounded the word. He pressed his hands to his breast pocket, then the pockets of his pants, and held them out again, palms up: I have nothing. Livy opened her mouth; her breathing was frighteningly loud. Her chest was heaving as if she'd been crying and she made a great effort to control it.

"What," she said.

"Help," he said.

He reached into his breast pocket, withdrew an object, and came closer, holding it out. She pointed the potato fork down at him. His obvious fatigue made him seem immovable, as if he had used all his strength to cross the yard and was therefore capable only of standing there forever. It was this that made her put out her hand and take the small flat object from him. He drew back instantly into himself, his shoulders going slack. She looked down at what she held in her hand: a plastic ID card, illegible in the dark, with a little square photo, and a bunch of folded money.

"What is this?" she said. "No, no. I don't want this. Take it back." She pushed it into his hand.

He accepted it, slowly, and put it back in his pocket. She could see that his chest was heaving now too, as if he'd been holding his breath. He pivoted on one foot and pointed across the yard to the garage. "House," he said.

"House?"

He pointed at his own chest, and then at the garage again. "House," he said. "I go." His hand flattened across his chest. The arm swung out and back. "Thank you," he said.

He turned and hurried away. She watched as he crossed the flat part of the yard, vanished briefly in the deep shadow of the privet bush, and then reappeared by the garage door. There was a moment of stillness, indistinct in the dark, possibly a minute struggle with the old latch, and then the door opened and he went inside.

Livy's mind rang like a bell. She picked up the cigarette where she had dropped it at her feet, put it out, and threw it under the porch stairs. Then she carried the potato fork to the far end of the porch and propped it against the wall.

She noticed that her hands were shaking. Her legs, when she stepped down into the grass, buckled under her. The grass was long and wet; it was a corner of the yard that had not been mowed in weeks, and she stayed on her knees in it for a minute, her fingers laced into the roots. Finally she got to her feet and walked around to the kitchen door. It was still unlocked. She went in and locked it behind her.

In the kitchen she drank a glass of water very fast and thought, *I have to go get the police right now.*

She stood at the sink with the empty glass. She could go downstairs and wake up her parents. They would get the police.

But she felt weak, almost faint. She went up to her bed and lay down. Her shoes were still on and after a while she sat up and pulled them off, which was more difficult than it normally was, as if her hands were numb. She sat with her hair falling in her face, trying to think. A little moonlight came in the window.

She lay down. She remembered a nightmare, which in her restive exhausted state felt like a cogent argument, a train of thought: herself on a sea choked with jostling ice, clinging to a floe that heaved and sank hideously.

She would get up and get her parents and the police.

But he looked so scared. He looked like her chemistry teachers: the glasses, the gray hair, the buttoned shirt. Many middle-aged men who worked indoors looked like this. She could think of a whole parade of them, wearing watches and windbreakers, teachers and restaurant managers and friends' fathers who worked in the city.

What would happen to him if the police found him? He looked like a man afraid for his life. She had heard things on TV about people like that disappearing. Foreign people who were taken to black sites. She had seen a documentary about it.

She wondered if he had killed someone. Many someones, maybe, to warrant all this. Her mind stalled there.

She fell asleep, somehow, curled up on her side.

3

He didn't sleep that night. It was pitch black inside the garage, and he sat down on a stack of lumber that he felt in the darkness and leaned against the wall and let his mind fade in and out for many hours. When light began to come through the windows he saw that there was a loft above him. He found a ladder and climbed up. The loft was full of old furniture.

He would have expected to feel anxious now, but he did not. He felt the calm of an infant—soft-brained, placid. He sat on the floor, leaning against a white-painted dresser. He'd turned everything over. He'd made his little bid. She might bring the police, but she might not. He was too tired and too hungry to care anymore.

He hoped that she might bring him something to eat. In a half-dreaming state, he developed a certainty that she would bring him an egg sandwich. It would have mayonnaise and soft cheese. He fell asleep as the sun was coming over the top of the hill, the valley floor still dark and cool. When he woke again and switched on his phone, there was a text message waiting for him in his own language:

Meet me in Pittsburgh.

※

Livy woke early and glanced automatically at her alarm clock. Its face was still blank, a rectangle of black overlaid with a faint redness. She guessed it was six. She had slept the remainder of the night in the same position, on her side with her face close to the cool plaster, and it took a minute of careful thought to remember what had happened. She felt around cautiously in her mind, staring hard at a drip in the paint on the wall.

The house was quiet and she needed to be out of it before her parents got up. They might not realize for a few hours that she wasn't in her room. She pulled her clothes on and hurried out the kitchen door, into the blue shade of a trellis of morning glories. The ground was damp. It had rained overnight. She walked around the corner of the house and looked out at the garage.

It was a gray pine building with a red tin roof, a storage place for furniture and garden tools, an old motorcycle that her father was perpetually looking to sell, several neglected bicycles, and a few stacks of lumber that had been left to season. They didn't keep the car in it; there was no room. As a child she had sometimes hidden in the loft and pretended it was her own house. Her parents were neighbors with whom she shared a driveway. When she went in to eat lunch, she was visiting. She was always doing this as a child, laying claim to parts of the house and yard. She loved things that were small and self-contained: dollhouses, crawl spaces. She loved to lock doors.

The garage looked as it always did. Honeysuckle vines choked the privet beside it. She had no idea what to do, but being alone with what she knew was intolerable. She turned and began to walk the route to Nelson's house.

It was very quiet in Lomath that morning; she saw no human movement all the way down Prospect Road. The sulfurous smell of burning plastic came from the far side of the creek. Ron Cash was up early, then, burning his trash.

She knocked on the Telas' front door and waited. Dry leaves had started to blow down from the trees. They were silted along the edge of the narrow concrete porch, which was otherwise clean; no one ever sat on it. There were no chairs. Mrs. Tela had asked Livy once about all the "things" in the Marko yard—lawn furniture, garden tools—out there for "anybody to take." Livy hadn't been sure at the time whether this was actually a rebuke about neatness or if it was just honest concern from a person who believed thieves were everywhere, a tide of thieves that would sweep away all loose objects.

There was an indistinct thud from behind the door and Livy heard Mrs. Tela's sharp voice say, "I said *do not*." There was another thumping noise and a quickly inhaled breath, and then the door jerked open and there was Nelson, off-balance, his glasses crooked, his mother a shadow in pajamas behind him.

"*Listen to me!*" she cried.

"It's just Livy," Nelson said. He was out of breath.

"You don't *listen to me!*" his mother said. She was crying. She moved right, trying to get past him: one long hand flashed out, reaching for the door. Nelson took hold of Livy's wrist and pulled her over the threshold. She stumbled into the room, not expecting this, her feet going out from under her. He slammed the door.

"You don't listen!" Mrs. Tela said. "It could be anybody out there!"

Nelson's sister Janine was sitting up on the sofa, where she had clearly slept: she was covered with a pink sheet, and a large pillow had slipped onto the floor. She stared at the three of them, her eyes half-closed.

"Stop it, Mom," she said.

Mrs. Tela looked at her, her face pink and wet, and then turned and disappeared into the dark hallway.

"So, we won't see her until lunch," Janine said. She lay back down.

Nelson watched his mother go down the hallway, then turned on his heel. "Hi," he said to Livy. He was standing with his hands on his hips, his elbows sticking out, catching his breath. "She chased me," he said.

"She was yanking on his shirt," Janine said from the sofa, her voice muffled. She was letting herself sink into the gap between the cushions and the back of the couch, her eyes closed, the bony backs of her wrists somewhere around her face.

"What's wrong with her?" Livy said.

"She doesn't want us to open the door."

Livy felt a sense of doom that was localized very precisely in the pit of her stomach. It was cold, concave. "I'm hungry," she said. "Do you have cereal?"

They went into the kitchen.

"My parents know we went to the pharmacy," Livy said. "I guess the word got out. Clarence told my dad."

"Fuck. Do they know about Mark?"

"No."

He rubbed his face, then took a long breath. "Well, we can't do anything. They'll find out or they won't." He turned away, rummaging for something to feed her. There was a box of something twig-like on a high shelf and a carton of soy milk—Janine was lactose-intolerant. There was a little yellow radio on the counter, encased in rubber, and he switched it on as he went by. Faint music, crackling and warm.

"Batteries?" Livy said.

"I found it in a closet yesterday."

"You're not listening to the news?"

"I got tired of it. They don't even know what country he's from. And the charges are secret."

"So what are you listening to? Zip 100?"

"Power 96. It's a crappy receiver, I can't get that much."

She listened to the music for a while. It was a song she disliked, but she recognized it without disappointment. She hadn't heard music in days—all car radios were tuned to the news, all the time. The girl singer sang about oceans of pain. It was so weird, Livy thought, that this rhyming description of vacillation over suicide had been set to a cheerful sing-along beat and was available on the radio for people in their cars. She felt that her normal life was an island retreating in the wake of a boat.

"Your cereal's getting mushy," Nelson said. "And my mom will completely lose her shit if she sees I gave you soy milk. You should eat it fast."

"Thanks."

He glanced at her from where he was standing in the doorway, keeping watch down the hall. "You're welcome."

"Do you think he's here?" She realized she had not asked him this yet. It had seemed, in a strange way, beside the point; they had enough to handle with the things they knew for sure. Now the question was a roundabout way of saying *Guess what?* The big surprises were always hard to spring.

"Who?" Nelson said.

"The guy they want."

"Not really. Why would he be?"

"Maybe it's a good place to hide?" she said.

"Evidently not, right?"

"Ha." She drew her spoon across the bottom of the ceramic bowl, listened to the high tone it made. "But you could see how a person might think it would be."

"Eat your cereal, seriously."

She lowered her head over the bowl. She didn't know what her strategy was. She wanted him to know, but the house made her doubt herself. It was both oppressive and flimsy, a drywall-and-fiberglass box on the open hillside with all the shades down. And Mrs. Tela's fear pervaded it like a gas. She had been right to try to block the door.

Livy looked at Nelson again, his back to her while he kept an eye on his mother's bedroom door. It struck her all at once that for days people had been speculating about whether the wanted person was in Lomath and who was helping him if he was, and it was her. Now when they talked in the store about this hypothetical betrayer, they were talking about her.

"Why'd you give me the milk, anyway?" she said.

He looked over his shoulder. "You said you were hungry."

The radio muttered the forecast: hot, hot, hot.

"Thanks," she said again.

She should have kept him out of the garage somehow. And why had he picked her? She couldn't think how to tell someone what had happened, and once she had given some of her trouble to Nelson she would not be able to get it back. He would be stuck there with her.

"Have you seen Mark?" Nelson said. He lowered his voice so Janine wouldn't hear.

"I did yesterday. He seemed okay." He actually seemed like an alien, a baffled organism blinking and shifting quietly in their midst. She rubbed her forehead. Was Mark afraid? The thought of causing anyone real fear was unbearable. "He was just hanging out, smoking on the porch roof. Didn't seem to think anyone would have noticed he was gone."

"Dominic and Brian are probably bored with the whole thing by now," Nelson said. "Maybe they'll just let him go."

"What'll happen then, though?" She imagined him walking away from the Spellar house, toward the line of barricades on Prospect Road. What would he say when he got there? How long would it take the police to come back, and who would they go looking for first?

"I don't know," Nelson said. "But the longer it goes on, the worse it's going to be."

"Right." She saw a chance to do something productive, to diminish slightly the pile of mistakes that had been mounting for the past two days. She could be the one to argue Dominic into ending this idiotic venture. She would talk sense into him. It hadn't worked yesterday, but today she would be more aggressive. "I'll go talk to him," she said, sitting up a little straighter.

"Okay." Nelson glanced over his shoulder at the dark hallway. "You want me to come with you? I could try to sneak out."

"No, that's okay." She drained the bowl and put it in the sink. "I'll see you later." She squeezed his arm reassuringly as she went by.

※

Livy walked back down the hill and skirted the intersection. She wondered if her parents were looking for her. They might assume for a while yet that she was staying sullenly in bed. Collier Road was all in shade. She noticed in the strengthening morning light that the shirt she was wearing, pulled carelessly from a pile on her floor, had a chain of pink stains across the front of it. She sucked her teeth in irritation at herself.

She let herself into the unlocked Spellar house, half-heartedly composing innocent explanations in case Lena might appear. *Oh I'm sorry, I didn't want to wake anybody up*. It was a reflex to cringe and fawn with adults; her parents had always been so casual with her that she overcompensated with other people's, fumbling for polite phrases like a traveler in a foreign country, sometimes applying a *Mr.* or *Mrs.* She knocked on Dominic's door at the top of the stairs.

There was a long silence. She put her mouth close to the doorframe and hissed through it. "*Dominic!*"

There was a rustling noise and the door opened. She stepped back without thinking; Dominic's size sometimes startled her. He was wearing basketball shorts.

"Sorry, you were sleeping," she said.

"No," he said. There were dark circles under his eyes, but he looked alert, almost painfully so. There was a sleeping bag on the floor, pushed half off a mat. Mark was asleep in the bed.

"You gave him the bed?" Livy said.

"Yeah . . ." He looked confused, as if she had caught him out. "He's, like, a guest."

"Is he still wearing the cuffs?"

"I took them off. They were pinching."

Mark suddenly turned on his side and spoke a few low, soft sentences in gibberish.

"I gave him some pills," Dominic said.

"What? What pills?"

"Klonopin, I think."

"What? Jesus, Dom!"

"He was just sitting with his back to the wall and staring. It was bothering the shit out of me. So I had these pills and I asked him if he wanted some and he said yeah. He's been sleeping since like eight last night." He ran his hand over his hair. "He smoked all my fucking cigarettes."

"Is he all right?"

"He's fine."

She walked around the bed and leaned over him. Her hair swung down over her shoulders and she held it back with both hands. She was very close to his face but wasn't sure what she was looking for. Breathing? She'd just heard him speak. His skin was pale, a little bluish, but he'd looked that way yesterday. There was a bit of white crust like toothpaste in the corners of his mouth. His brow wrinkled slightly in his sleep, as if he'd perceived her breathy heat. She straightened and turned away.

"He's fine," Dominic said again. "What do you want?"

"Nothing. I just wanted to check up on things. Over here." She looked at him. "People know we went. I guess you know that."

"Yeah, I told my mom. I couldn't really give her the medicine otherwise."

"But you didn't tell them we stole it."

"No, I didn't tell them we stole it."

Maybe he was the person to tell about the man in the garage. He had shuffled over to his dresser and she watched him push things around in the second drawer. He had a broad, square back, freckled like hers at the shoulders, a half-moon of sunburn on the neck. It almost felt like it wouldn't matter if she told him—he was in worse trouble himself. But that was a bad idea. Dominic would keep things together only as long as it was easier than letting them fall apart. She watched him shrug himself into a T-shirt, cautious with his bulk, like a van backing into a parking space.

"The state cops are leaving," he said, heaving the drawer shut. "It's all federal now, and Maronne PD."

"Who said?"

"My mom. She was out last night talking to people."

"Is that better or worse?"

He looked over his shoulder at her and chuckled.

"Does that mean you know, or you don't know?" she said, annoyed.

"It means it's a stupid question, I don't know." He leaned against the dresser. "You're scared. So is Brian. He keeps coming over and checking up, too."

"The cops are going to find out," Livy said. "You should just let him go." She tried to catch his eyes, to communicate how seriously she meant it, but he evaded her easily.

"I'll let him go." He looked at Mark, rubbing his lower lip. "At the right time."

Livy laughed. "When is that going to be?"

"When nobody's looking. When everybody's running around losing their shit. Then I'll let him go and nobody will notice."

"What are you talking about?" Livy said. He just stood there, expecting terrible things to happen. She wanted to shove him. "This is your fault, Dom," she said. "You are more fucked than the rest of us. He's in your house and it was your gun and your idea. You should let him go now."

"I can't."

"You can't *keep* him either!"

"If this is just my problem, then get the fuck out, why don't you?"

She stepped back, her feet shuffling in the carpet. "You're making it—"

"Get the fuck *out*, Livy." He waved at the door behind her. She stared at him, trying to think of something more to say, but he rolled his eyes and turned his back. She left, closing the door with a click behind her.

A cloud of failure settled over her. She hesitated when she reached the bright front yard, one hand on the latch of the decorative gate, and then edged around the side yard and into the back. The backyard was shaded by tall, ragged walnut trees. She walked down to the water, passing the gazing ball that she liked, and stood still on the muddy bank, listening hard in all directions. A pit bull in the neighbor's yard stood up with a gentle rattle of chain and came close to the fence, watching Livy with its head down, feet planted, tail wagging slightly. *Why is no one in the world afraid of me?* Livy thought. *Even a dog on a chain doesn't get its back up.* Strange children were always coming up to her and offering their laces for her to tie. She thought that this was why the man had picked her: she looked soft. And he'd been right. It was hard for her to remember now why she hadn't yelled when he handed her his things, why she hadn't kept banging on the door until her parents woke up. She was losing the logic of it.

She waded across the creek, swinging her hands out in stiff arcs to balance the slog. The far side was covered

in a crackle of leaves. She climbed up the steep bank to
the road, dirt cascading into her shoes, and stopped in
the lee of the bridge wall.

She could see the police at the turn in the road, and
it looked like Dominic and his mother were right: the
van was a different color now, dark blue instead of white,
and there was another one idling behind it, almost out of
sight behind the trailing branches of a lightning-struck
tree. More federal people. There was a buzzing in the air.
She tried for a while to fix on it, but found that it faded
when she tried hardest to hear: a hum of radios, she
guessed, coming to her down a favorable corridor of air.

This was how she could fix the problem of the man
in the garage: she could climb out from behind the wall
and walk down to where the police were. There were
three of them standing around the van, and they looked
different today: two were in ordinary clothes, polo shirts
and jeans, and the other wore a tan uniform, the shirt
unbuttoned, a white undershirt beneath. She could tell
them, and they would come get the man, and the whole
problem would be over for all of them, maybe.

Or the police would take an interest in her, they
would walk through her yard and question her parents
and friends, and they would find Mark.

She sat down in the leaves. She had a sudden sense
of the aloneness of her body, her flesh containing itself:

she extended no farther than her shoes in one direction, no farther than her hair in the other. She pressed her shoulders and the back of her head against the wall and braced her arms across her knees. She closed her eyes, trying to think.

After a while hunger drove her to cross the creek again and walk up to the store. The door was propped open.

"You look sick," Jocelyn said. "Are you sick?"

Jocelyn looked sick herself; her hands were flat on the counter, as if she needed the help to stay on her feet, and her hair was stuck to pale temples.

"I'm okay," Livy said.

"Ron's talking about doing another house-to-house search," Jocelyn said. "We could do it better than they can. They're working from maps, have you seen that? I saw them standing right in front here yesterday"—she pointed at the door—"looking at a map. I wanted to tell them, you can see most of it from where you're standing, you don't need a map."

Livy's face was red and damp. Heat radiated from her armpits. How could her body be so obvious? "Ron wants to search the houses?"

"Yes he does." Jocelyn leaned against the wall. Her eyes narrowed when she drew on her cigarette; Livy could see some deep satisfaction in her face that could have been either the cigarette or the prospect of action.

Jocelyn tilted her head from side to side, slowly, as if trying to loosen her muscles, and placed her hand on the back of her neck. "Get this over with, you know."

"Right," Livy said. Her sweating and blushing were becoming indiscreet. She turned abruptly and walked out, stumbling on the steps outside. The weeds at the side of the road scratched at her legs, left burrs in her jeans. She fell into a breathless, knock-kneed run down the slope of Collier Road, a kind of controlled fall, her hands paddling the air. She was alone in the bright morning. The vast, still roof of the Sportsmen's Club glittered in the sun. She was too hot. She ran for the water.

There was a catwalk along the Black Rock Creek at the foot of the club wall. She turned onto it and ran to the end. Her legs were hot, and cold, and twitching. She pulled off her shoes, climbed over the iron railing, and dropped into the water. Her knees buckled and she sat down hard on the stones and fell back, drawing in a breath. She let the water drag her down, fill her clothes, and lift her up again. When she raised her head a squirrel was watching her from the top of the wall.

She kept still and the fish came almost immediately. She felt them slipping past her feet. A mouth bumped gently, quizzically, against her wrist. She closed her eyes. She couldn't tell the police. She couldn't stomach it; he looked so afraid, and she didn't trust any of them, the

Maronne Police Department or the FBI or the CIA, all
the people Ron Cash said were there. She couldn't tell
her parents because they, being adults, would tell the police. And she couldn't leave him there, pretend she was
unaware of him, and hope he would leave, because Ron
would be coming with a search party.

Her mind cascaded with other things she couldn't
do. This was her strong suit. She was good at seeing
pitfalls. But then, of course, she went and did things
anyway. Her fingers dug between the stones. She held
herself in place.

※

She stood in the creek just behind her parents' garden, listening hard, in case her father or mother was nearby. She
had waded up through the shallow rocky stretches of the
Black Rock so she might reach the garage unobserved.

The back of the garage provoked her with its stillness, its largeness and grayness. *Sometimes in life*, she
thought. *And, you know, you just have to*— She didn't finish the thought. Her inner voice chattered in a fitful,
ill-tempered shorthand. A yellow cat, matted and plod-
ding, appeared on the surging sycamore roots at the top
of the bank. He belonged to one of the neighbors up the
road. He glanced at her and then walked away around

the trunk of the tree, causing a shiver in the jewelweed as he disappeared.

There seemed to be no one else around. She climbed the bank on her hands and knees and sat up cautiously at the top. She was half-hidden behind a stack of bricks covered with a tarp. The yard was miraculously empty.

She darted for the back of the garage and edged around to the door, which was visible from the house. The latch clattered open in her hands and clattered shut behind her. Inside was the familiar creosote smell, the cool scent of damp undisturbed gravel, the spider webs backlit against the windows.

It took a few seconds for her eyes to adjust, and in that time she stood in near-total darkness, unable to hear over her own breathing. The room appeared around her by imperceptible degrees. There was the rototiller, the stacks of lumber. The man wasn't there. She edged to the back of the garage to be sure, peering into the deeper darkness under the loft. There was nothing there but rakes and shovels and coils of hose hung on a nail.

She felt a wave of relief. Her tight breathing relaxed and she took several deep gasping breaths that came out like guffaws. There was a noise in the loft above her.

The ladder was there. Ordinarily it leaned against the back wall, but here it was, propped against the edge of the loft. Her breathing ceased again. "Hello?" she said.

She heard nothing. "Hey," she said, her voice meandering in pitch like a saw blade bending. "Come down, please." There was no response. She argued with herself for several minutes at the foot of the ladder, trying to think of an alternative to climbing it; she had to talk to him but the prospect made her nervous. She went up anyway, awkwardly bowlegged, keeping her knees out of the way. He was there, in front of the ladder, an arm's length away.

"Hi," she said.

He was sitting against an old dresser, a pink-and-white thing with tiny flowers that had been in her room when she was little. His eyebrows were raised behind his round glasses and his hair was still standing up.

"Hi," she said again.

"Hello," he said. He had to try it twice; the first time it caught in his throat, as if it were the first time he'd spoken that day. It probably was. He glanced at her wet hair. She pushed it back out of her face.

"You're still here," she said.

His tense, open expression did not change. He shifted his gaze from her left eye to her right, then back again, then stopped.

"Can you understand me?" she said.

"No English."

"But you understood what I just asked you?"

"No understand."

"You don't understand?"

"No English," he said. He splayed the fingers of one hand in the air, frowning down at it.

"You have to go," she said. "People are coming." Again he looked at each of her eyes in turn, then appeared to control the impulse and returned to a general observation of her face. He was frowning, focusing.

"They're coming, you have to go," she said again. Why repeat it? Why keep talking at all? "Are you hungry?" She put her hand on her stomach, made a face of discomfort, pointed at him. "Hungry?"

He put his hand on his stomach. "Yes."

Her skin prickled. There was something dislocated here, something unfamiliar to her. Then she realized what it was. "Are you scared of me?" she said.

His expression, again, did not change. She pointed at him, then at her own chest. "Scared? Afraid?" She laughed, a too-loud trill. "Okay." She rubbed her forehead. That was what it was before, when she let him give her his money and ID for a minute: it was the fear in his face. She was slight and narrow-wristed; people often backed into her in the hallways at school without seeing her, stepped on her feet, knocked into her with elbows, looking over her head. Even skinny Nelson was broader than she was in the shoulders and could, without comment, open stuck doors and lift window sashes she had no effect on. Revaz was trying to read her face. He was looking clearly and intently at her, and it was because she spoke the language and knew the terrain and could ruin him if she wanted.

"You have to go," she said again.

"Go," he said. He took a cell phone from his pocket, which surprised her. "I go *this*," he said, tapping the glowing screen, and she saw a scramble of letters and then *Pittsburgh*, emerging from the chaos. He underlined the city's name with his finger. "This."

"You need to go to Pittsburgh? That's hundreds of miles away."

"This." He tapped again.

"Do you know people there?"

He leaned back against the dresser.

"Okay," she said. "I'll help you." She was trying it out. He didn't understand her anyway, and couldn't hold her to it. "There's a train. You could get the train in Cooverton and take it to Pittsburgh. Where are you from?"

He shook his head.

"How did you get here? How long has it been since you ate anything?"

He unclasped his hands from his knees and sat back against the dresser. He appeared to be drifting away from her, perhaps understanding that she was not really speaking to him anymore.

"I'm hungry too," she said. "I can't go in my house." She dug in her pants pocket, holding on to the ladder with her other hand. "I have four dollars," she said. "But I don't want to have to talk to Jocelyn." She felt the inertia of the garage, the heaviness in the air. The two of them were a stone that had rolled to the bottom of a hill. Nothing would shift without an enormous effort on her part, a long push up a slope.

"Stay here and be quiet," she said. She put her finger to her lips. "It's just me." She squinted at him, as if this would convey her meaning. "But maybe I could tell my friend. Should I tell my friend? You don't know."

A mouse stared at her from beneath the dresser. She saw it just to the right of the man, its perfect black eyes, its perfect composure beside the scalloped wooden leg. Then it was gone.

"I have to go," she said. "I have to think. I'll be back later."

This seemed important, this last thing, and impossible to express. How could you mime the future tense? How could you suggest return? She pointed to herself, walked her fingers away in the air, made them pause and consider and come walking back. His face was inscrutable.

※

"Nelson," she said. She was standing outside his bedroom window, having decided not to brave the front door again. "Are you there?"

There was some rustling, cloth on cloth, and then he appeared in the window.

"Were you sleeping?" she said.

He rubbed his eyes. "Just lying in bed." *Liar*, she thought. He leaned closer to the screen, squinting at her. "Are you wet?" he said.

"Yes." She crossed her arms.

"Why are you all wet?" He laughed and started to tug at the screen, which squeaked as the flimsy metal pieces scooted over each other. It occurred to Livy that her whole day was animal-like, the way she'd been creeping through backyards and huddling in the water. Like a groundhog or muskrat or mouse. The creek had always been the most direct route from her house to the neighbors', safer than the roads, and shorter. Nelson, now that she thought about it, was the only friend she'd ever had in Lomath whose house wasn't next to the Black Rock Creek. Her childhood friends, at the age when nothing really mattered in a friendship beyond proximity and whether you were the kind of kid who threw rocks or the kind of kid who didn't, were the Green twins and the DiLorenzos next door and the Caffertys on the other side of the driveway—the Black Rock winding past all their doors. They wore paths into the weeds along its banks, walking between their houses. The Caffertys and DiLorenzos had moved a few years ago and the Green twins were no longer friendly at school; mysterious divisions arose between white kids and black kids in junior high and did not diminish as the years passed. Around the time the Caffertys and the DiLorenzos and the Green twins were disappearing, there was Nelson, stranded on his hill. An encore friend, childhood part two, the boy who'd come to keep her company when everyone else had gone.

"I was hot." She looked down at her wet jeans. "These are uncomfortable, actually. Can I—"

"Yeah, hold on." He stepped away from the window, and then he was back, pulling the screen out of the frame, holding a pair of gym shorts. "What's on your shirt?"

She looked at the stain. "I don't know," she said. "It's not from today." She reached for the shorts.

"You're going to change out there?"

She glanced behind her, down the bright empty slope of the yard. "Maybe I should come in, actually," Livy said. She climbed over the sill and worked her feet out of her shoes without undoing the laces. She thought to ask Nelson to turn his back, but he had already done it, and seemed engrossed in the covers of the books in a cascading pile beside his door. She worked the wet jeans down her cold thighs. The creases in the fabric were printed on the backs of her knees in pink and white.

"I'm taking this shirt, too, if you don't mind," she said, picking one up off the floor.

"Go for it." He knelt down and began to read the back of the stumpy copy of *David Copperfield* sticking out from under his bed, which Livy knew was an assigned text from their English class two years ago and of no interest to him at all. She looked down at herself, wobbling on one foot with the other stuck in the lining of the borrowed nylon shorts: bluish goose-bumped flesh and a bra that had turned from tan to pale orange in the wash. She pulled the shirt on over her head.

"You can turn around," she said.

He glanced at her.

"I want to tell you something but I don't know if I should," she said.

"Did something happen with Mark?" His eyes were wide.

"No, it's not him, he's fine." She rubbed the hinge of her jaw with the tips of her fingers. It was sore, as if she'd been hit, or had ground her teeth all night. "It could be a lot of trouble," she said. "So if you don't want me to tell you, just say so now, please."

Nelson's shoulders were slack and his hand hovered near his chin. This was his most attentive expression. The pause stretched out. "How much more trouble can it be?" he said finally.

"The guy the cops are looking for is at my house," she said. "I was out in the yard and he came out of the woods and gave me everything in his pockets and then just walked into the garage."

They stared at each other as if each were equally surprised. There was a rush and hum in the walls as someone turned the water on in the kitchen. A scratch sounded at the door, and Livy jumped, feeling the muscles tighten all down her back.

Nelson recovered his power of speech. "It's just the cat," he said. He glanced at the door, moved to open it, decided not to. "You're sure it's him?"

She nodded.

"Fuck," he said. "What are we going to do?"

She absorbed the word *we*. He took his glasses off. He did that when people argued near him, she had seen him do it many times. The tension would rise in the room and he would reach up casually and blind himself.

"I have to get him out of there," Livy said, her voice quavering a little. "Ron wants to search all the houses again."

"He does? What are we going to do about Mark?"

"Christ, I don't know."

He put his glasses back on. "What is he like? Beni or Deni or whatever his name is?"

She made a vague arc in the air with her hand. "He's like the picture. He looks like a businessman. Or a teacher. He doesn't speak English."

"Did he threaten you?"

"He doesn't speak English, I said."

"Yeah, but—" He flung his hand out, splayed his fingers.

"He didn't. He was begging me, basically."

"You can't tell where he's from?"

"No." She went over to the window, where she had dropped her shoes on the carpet. "I have to get him out. I don't want to give him to the police, I just—I just don't. But they can't find him here either. I already let him stay overnight in the garage. That's bad. He wants to go to Pittsburgh."

"Do you think he did something serious?"

"I don't know. I don't know." She stared at the dark computer monitor on the other side of the room. She closed her eyes. "I'm just going to get him out. I'm going to put him on a bicycle." She had been turning this single idea over in her mind for an hour, waiting for a better one to come to her.

"A bicycle?" Nelson said, looking up. "He'll . . . pedal away?"

"Well, it's better than walking, and it's not like I can drive him out. My mom never rides her bike. I can pump up the tires and take him over the hill with it and put him on the trail, and then from there he can get onto 72 and he won't be our problem anymore. I've done it myself a couple of times."

"So you're going to go over the hill with him? In the dark?"

"Yeah."

"They'll catch you with him," Nelson said, alarm in his face. "You know how much trouble you'd be in? That's jail, that's *real* jail."

"There might not be any cops over that way," she said. It seemed important now that her plan be deemed solid and reasonable. "There's no road there, just the trail."

"I'll take him," Nelson said. His eyes were very wide, dense and dark.

"What? That doesn't make any sense. Why should you do it instead of me?" They were dressed alike now, both in T-shirts and gym shorts. She saw herself for a second as a squeaking, presuming child, arms crossed, advancing a dubious strategy.

"So we're both going, then," he said.

Something in her shoulders relaxed when he said it. She realized now that this was why she had come. She was hoping for the company, even though she couldn't have asked, because it was an outrageous thing to ask for. "What if your mom catches you leaving?" she said, hedging, looking just to the right of his face.

"Don't worry about it."

She hugged him abruptly. She smelled sweat and an edge of lemony deodorant. "I need a flashlight," she said into his T-shirt. "Do you have an extra one?"

He went to his desk and produced a key chain flashlight. "I'll come meet you when it gets dark," he said, palming it into her hand.

"Okay," she said. She shrugged as she said it, but tears were stinging her eyes. She pretended to examine the light. "Thanks."

※

She saw them as she came down Collier: her parents on the front steps of the store, talking to Jocelyn and Noreen. Her mother was biting her lip. Livy backed behind a boxwood hedge and sank down into the grass. Jocelyn was pointing up Collier and Noreen was rubbing Livy's mother's back. Livy's guilt rose up again; she hated to make her parents worry. They were so reasonable most of the time. She backed away from the hedge and ducked around the side of a small yellow house and into the woods.

There was no cleared path there and she got herself tangled in a multiflora rosebush only a few feet into the trees. It took several minutes to get herself unstuck from it, tearing her shirt, leaving powdery white scratches on her arms. This close and meticulous work, unhooking the thorns, calmed her down, and once she was free of the rosebush she sat down on a stone to wait. Twenty minutes, half an hour, and her parents would have knocked on the Telas' door, found she wasn't there, and gone off someplace else to look for her. She would only have to wait. She wished she had a watch.

The rosebush protected her. No one would come through this way. She sat for a while with her head on her knees, breathing as slowly as she could.

What if he'd done something serious? she thought. Nelson's question. What if he had?

Get him out of here, she thought. *Out of here, out of here, out of here.*

※

Revaz had thought she would come back right away with something to eat. She had asked if he wanted food, unless he had somehow grossly misunderstood her. But hours passed, and she didn't come back.

He needed something to do with his hands. He opened the cedar-scented drawers of the dresser one by one. In the bottom one, there were forty-five cents and a child's sock with a ruffle at the ankle. Under the windows there were boxes full of books, and he passed the time for a while by lifting them out and looking at the covers and then putting them back very carefully where they belonged. They were mostly paperbacks, including ten that obviously belonged to a series and all had dreamy paintings of young women on them, clutching books to their chests, wearing Edwardian dresses.

She hadn't come back with food but she also hadn't come back with the police. She might be planning to help him. It was possible.

These were probably her books, put away now because she was too old for them. He had a goddaughter who was fifteen, a nice girl. He felt sad at the thought of her. He guessed that this girl was sixteen or seventeen, although he'd never been good at guessing the ages of children. She was pretty (all girls that age were pretty). She was freckled and had long, loose hair.

If she hadn't brought the police by now, she would not bring them.

Were women naturally empathetic? He was old-fashioned in believing they were. He straightened his stiff knee, painfully, until he was sitting with his legs sticking out in front of him like a child. He'd always believed women would come and save him, and usually one did. Girlfriends here and there. His sister, until she was gone.

✳

After a while—half an hour or forty-five minutes, she couldn't tell—Livy slipped down through the woods to White Horse Road. She would have to wait until dark to retrieve the bike, she realized now. Queen Anne's lace was blooming along the road, half strangled in nets of crown vetch. In June she had walked here with Nelson, picking wineberries, ducking out of the way of passing cars. She walked on the yellow stripe in the middle now. A gust of wind had knocked a few bright leaves loose from the trees and they lay here and there in bunches on the road, undisturbed.

Where the road turned, just before the roadblock came into sight, she sat down in the dirt by the guardrail. A pair of white butterflies looped in the still air over the asphalt. She had hours of daylight to wait through.

The Markos sometimes went back to camp at the farm where Livy's parents had once lived. The old fields were wild now, the house had been annexed by hornets and mice, and the yard was a thicket with stray poppies staggering through it. Once Livy had gotten up in the middle of the night to pee and the silence outside the tent had astonished her. There was no wind and no highway, no water running by, and after using the outhouse she'd stood outside for a long time listening, arms crossed, barefoot.

The silence had been so complete it felt like deafness. There was a strange pressure in her ears, as if they had been switched off or blocked. She stood on packed earth; the grass grew knee-high beside the bare patch, and each blade of it, each angled stem and puff of seed, was perfectly still. She began to hear her own blood hissing in her ears. She looked at the edge of the woods, the field going over the hill, the stand of walnut trees around the bedrock at the top, and none of it scratched out any sound to match the seething in her veins. Her aliveness was monumental, and the world was faint and distant and dark.

She had been like that for most of her adolescence, vivid to herself with the world muted and blurred around her. Now the world was thunderous. She pulled up a blade of grass and chewed on the end of it. The world was loud and close, and her heart and lungs and brain were a tinny afterthought.

※

It was seven thirty before the sky began to dim. Livy was waiting it out behind the Sportsmen's Club, on the patch of grass where the last manager had been thinking, shortly before he quit, about setting up some tables and patio umbrellas. He had used the words *alfresco*. The patch of grass was pleasant, but it was small and it faced the back of the building, a carelessly stuccoed wall with a heavy metal door in it, painted brown. It had seemed to

Livy, when he suggested it, like an indication of the gap between the kind of restaurant he thought he deserved and the one he was in.

There was never much of a sunset in Lomath. The hills were in the way and all they got were side effects, an orangeness in the air. Livy had been moving around all day and her fear of encountering her parents was so intense that it was funny: it made her feel like a small child again, a kid on TV who had broken a lamp. Birds animated a tree across the parking lot, an invisible mob in the upper branches. She waited and waited.

✳

She realized, crossing the creek in the new dark, that Revaz must be thirsty. He was hungry too, but she still couldn't go into her own house to get anything to eat, and thirst was more of a problem. She pictured him unconscious, an enormous unshiftable weight. There were jars in the garage. The hose might be unspooled in the garden; if she was lucky her father might have forgotten to turn the valve off in the house.

Her house looked dark from across the yard. Her parents might have been home or not; lit candles were invisible from outside. She hurried around the corner of the garage and pushed open the door.

"Hello?" she said. "Sir?"

The dark was close and it felt populated. She dug in her pocket for the key chain flashlight Nelson had given her. It was small, encased in soft plastic; she squeezed it and the little light came on. She found a carpenter pencil in an old baking soda can and pocketed it. The big canning jars were on the shelf by the door. She took one and backed out of the garage again, found the hose lying among the rhubarb, filled the jar, drank half of it down, then filled it again. The water was warm and smelled like rubber, but it was the best she could do.

Back in the garage she repeated herself. "Hello?"

She heard something like a shoe scraping on the boards of the loft. "Hello," he said.

She aimed the flashlight at the loft. There were indistinct shapes, a gleam of white paint.

"I brought you water," she said.

He said nothing. Why did she keep talking to him? She crossed carefully to the ladder and climbed it. The full jar made her hand ache. "Water," she said.

He was sitting against the north-facing wall, one ear visible in the light from the window. She set the jar down on the boards and pushed it toward him. He heaved himself onto his knees and reached for it. "Thank you," he said. He lifted it clumsily and water poured down his chin.

"Sorry it's warm," Livy said. She could hear his throat working. She looked away. "Sorry I didn't think of it before."

He set the empty jar down. "Thank you," he said again.

"Map," she said. She pretended to unfold and refold a map several times, and at last he pulled the map from his pocket and handed it to her. "We're going to get you out tonight," she said. She had an urge to point the flashlight at him. It was strange to talk to someone whose face she couldn't see. "I have a bicycle—bike, bike . . ." She gestured meaninglessly. He would see the one downstairs in a minute anyway. "A bike for you to ride. We'll take it over the hill and you'll go down a trail to a highway." She unfolded the map on the floor and drew in the trail with a thick stroke of the carpenter pencil. They would go over the hill, and then he would ride down the trail, which followed the Lomath Creek for half a mile before crossing it on an old railroad bridge and continuing across flat bottomlands to the highway.

"Here," she said. "We go to the trail, and you go down the trail to the highway, and you turn left," she said. She traced the highway with the pencil, finished in Cooverton with a triumphant flourish. "To Cooverton. Where there's a train. To Pittsburgh." She sketched a train, an arrow, the magic word: *Pittsburgh*.

"I go," he said.

Did that mean he understood? "Okay, good," she said. "Good good good."

Her face was hot with nerves, her forehead was slick. She backed down the ladder. The bike was hanging on a hook back under the loft, and it took her several minutes of sweating and cursing in the dark to get it untangled from the rakes that hemmed it in. It came free finally with a clanking of pedals, and the tires hit the gravel floor of the garage with no resistance at all. Her heart sank.

"The tires are flat," she called up to the man in the loft. It was reflexive to talk, and the more complete the silence of the other party was, the more she was driven to narrate. She was the same way with babies. She shined the flashlight around in the mess. She saw a pump gleaming on a nail beside the rakes.

There was some shuffling upstairs. The man's head appeared over the edge. "Okay?" he said.

"Okay." She did a thumbs-up, invisible in the dark. She had to hold the flashlight in her mouth while she pumped up the tires. They held air. This was the luckiest thing that had ever happened. She flipped the bike over so it was propped on its seat and turned the pedals a few times with her hand, and the wheels spun solidly, heavily, and made the correct noise. She was flushed with success.

"Hey," she said. She shined the flashlight into the loft and beckoned. "Come down."

She heard the boards creak, a quick exhale and shifting of weight. He climbed very slowly down the ladder.

"Bike," she said. "For you." She put her hand on the wheel, which was still spinning. "You ride?" She turned the bike over, patted the seat. "Can you ride? You know how to ride? You go to Cooverton," she said, holding up the map again, "on this," pointing to the bike. "Okay?" she said. She patted the seat energetically.

With one hand Revaz loosened the crank on the seat and raised it a few inches.

"Okay!" she said. "You understand!"

"Okay," he said. He tightened the crank, loosened it, straightened the seat, tightened it again.

"Yes, good!" she said. "It was too low for you!"

She went and stood by the door, listening. She heard nothing in particular coming from outside. "My friend is coming to meet us," she said over her shoulder.

Revaz was squeezing the tires. He seemed satisfied with them. He lifted the bike slightly by the handlebars and dropped it on the gravel once, twice, three times, so it bounced. He ran his fingers over the chain and then wiped the grease on his pants.

"We'll wait a little bit," Livy said.

He rolled the bike forward and back on the gravel, forward and back. He was waiting for her to do something—that was why he was standing there making meaningless assessments of the bike. Demonstratively, Livy settled down on the lumber to wait, her knees jiggling with nerves. Revaz put the kickstand down with one foot and stood with his hands in his pockets. He had a heavy kind of patience, standing very still.

There was a tension in Livy's abdomen that pulled at the rest of her body. She sifted the night sounds for footsteps, but heard nothing. Acid was thickening in her stomach. An interval crept by that felt like twenty minutes, or ten, or an hour. Had Nelson forgotten? It was unlikely. Maybe he'd been prevented from leaving, or stopped on the way, or maybe it was just too hard to arrange a meeting with no clocks. Her cell phone battery was dead and so was his. He'd said he would come when it was dark, and it was dark now, had been dark for a little while already. The minutes felt viscous, stretching and sticking; the effect got worse the more she tried to track the time.

"We should just go," she said finally. She heard Revaz shift on the gravel, perhaps looking at her, but it was too dark to see him clearly. She took a couple of deep breaths, her legs tensing, and allowed for a few last-minute intercessions: Nelson could knock softly at the door now, or now, or now. But there was nothing.

"All right," she said, standing up. She tried to shrug off her disappointment, pack it away. "Now." She pulled open the door. The blackness gave way to the yard in weak moonlight. She pulled the bike out of Revaz's hands and walked out into the grass and around the side of the building. She kept her head up, her hair bouncing in a silly girlish way on the back of her neck. The grass was soaked with dew. She walked fast but did not yet permit herself to run. She heard him close the door behind him, quickly but softly.

"Okay," he stage-whispered, hurrying after her.

Livy dragged the bike through the creek and clambered up the far bank. Revaz followed, breathing audibly. His white shirt was terribly visible in the moonlight.

"Okay," Livy muttered to herself, uncontrollably. "Okay. Okay." She began to run, drawing in great dilating breaths. Revaz fell into a jog behind her. The woods were dark and still, but Livy could see very clearly. The bike rattled and bashed against her legs as she rounded the turn by the Inskys' long driveway. The moon was high and through the trees that lined the road she could see the Inskys' pastures rolling away below her, smooth as cream. There was no wind. It took less than five minutes to reach the top of the hill, and there the road ended at a fence. There was a well-worn path around the gate, and Livy slowed to a walk to guide the bike through it. Revaz stopped and coughed once or twice.

She waited on the other side of the gate for him to catch up. He was unsteady, as if carrying another person on his shoulders. He put one hand on the top bar of the fence and took a few deep scraping breaths.

"Are you all right?" Livy said. She didn't know how long it had been since he'd eaten. He might have asthma, a weak heart. His chest was heaving as it had been when she first encountered him, and his mouth was open. She put the kickstand down on the bike and came back to the gate. "Are you okay?" she said. She touched his arm.

"Okay," he said.

The top of the hill was bare. In normal times boys rode four-wheelers and dirt bikes across the open space and into the woods farther down. On a bright night like this it felt like a stage, held up broad and flat above the trees and distant houses and the highway that girdled the Lomath valley. It was a dangerous place to be.

"We have to hurry," she said. "We can't stand here." She grabbed the bike and jogged away from him. It veered in her hands and she banged her shin on it. "Come on, please," she said to him. Ahead there was an open strip thirty yards wide where the trees had been cleared, years before, for easy access to the sewer lines beneath. It ran from the top of the hill to the bottom. Livy headed for it. "It's downhill from here," she hissed over her shoulder. "It's easy."

He followed her, jogging gamely, with more movement in his arms than in his legs. She watched her feet as well as she could; the ground was difficult, strewn with gravel knocked down by the dirt bikes, marked with unexpected ditches where the water cut through when it rained too hard. The plumes of seeded grasses whipped her legs. As she stepped over a branch in the path, a light flashed at the corner of her eye. She turned her head to see where it had come from and fell.

She had not fallen like this since she was little. She somersaulted; the bike was wrenched from her hands and she went down first on her left forearm, then her face, and then flipped over, her feet slashing through the air, and landed on her back so hard the air was knocked out of her lungs.

She opened her eyes, struggling for breath, and Revaz was crouching over her, whispering incomprehensible words.

Her lungs opened and pulled. "Shiiiit," she whispered.

He disappeared from view and then he was back, tugging on her arms. She could feel her legs now, her back, her feet, and it was all ringing and thudding. She half turned while he pulled her and tried to get up onto her knees, and both of them tipped over. The bike wheels spun nearby.

"I'm okay," she whispered. "My head."

Her head was ringing and thudding harder than anything else; it was the source of the ringing and thudding. Her shaking arms gave out and she sank down. Distinct pains were beginning to emerge. Her cheek and forehead stung. A powerful throbbing issued from the lower ribs in her back, on the right side. She was grateful to be on the ground.

She lay with her face in the dirt, resting on the unscraped side. Small insects crawled on her legs.

"There was a light," she said.

Revaz was a mass to her left, sitting and waiting. She pushed herself onto her knees, very slowly, accounting for all the parts of her body. She felt a little better. The pain was focused now at a few fixed points and had withdrawn from the interstices of her head and back and belly. She got to her feet. She saw that the flashlight, which she had clipped to her waistband, was on. It had a pulse setting and it was flashing away, swinging back and forth on its short chain.

"Oh," she said. "It was just . . ." She looked at him. "I thought I saw a light, but it was just this." She pointed at it. He looked confused. "No light!" she said. She started to laugh, but it made her head hurt.

They walked the rest of the way down. Livy felt calm; her blood was a soup of numbing chemicals. The air was sweet and cool. In a few minutes they stepped down into the sand and mud at the bottom of the hill, on the often-flooded margin of the Lomath Creek. Tussocks of grass interrupted the eroding bank. Livy veered off to the right, toward the trail that Revaz would take.

The trail was broad and flat, and it followed the creek on a shelf that had been carved out for the railroad a long time ago. That particular line, which had once connected two mills, had been out of use since before Livy was born, and when the rails were pulled out and the ties rotted away, a broad gravel pathway was left behind. These paths appeared here and there in the woods around Maronne, connecting it to other towns with straight industrial lines. Livy came to the mouth of the trail.

"This is it," she said.

She put the bike's kickstand down. Her fingers were stiff. She tried to squeeze the little light on and it flipped out of her hands.

"The map, the map," she said. She mimed unfolding, and he stared at her and then produced the map from his pocket again. She tried to flatten it out in the beam of the flashlight. "You go here," she said. She traced the line with her finger, from the creek to the highway. "Road," she said, pointing at Route 72. "East, west."

The bike was between them. He folded the map and put it in his breast pocket, and then took several bills from his pocket and held them out to her.

"No, no," she said. What would she want his money for? He looked at her several times, then put the money carefully back in his pocket. He rolled the bike to the end of the path, glanced back at her again, and then pointed ahead, into the dark.

"Yes," she said.

He looked into the darkness of the trees for a few seconds, holding the bike.

"Okay," he said. "Thank you."

She'd always imagined a person would know, at a time like this, whether they were doing a good thing or a bad thing. But all she knew was that it was difficult, and that she wished she didn't have to do it. She looked into the dark with him.

He got on the bike and it wobbled a little and then he was gone. The noise of the tires persisted, and then that was gone too. She stood for a second and listened. There was nothing: no one was coming. She kept expecting to hear police radios, footsteps from the top of the hill, but there was no sound but the creek and the crickets in the high grass.

She walked back up the hill instead of running. It was too steep and she felt clumsy and numb. She wasn't sure how long it had been since she left the garage. Ten minutes? Half an hour? The sky was a strange color, a deep transparent blue to the west, over a distant hilltop crowned with a subdivision.

At the top of the hill she skirted the open area, walking in the shadow of the trees until she reached the gate. Once she was on the road she relaxed a little. She paused at the Inskys' fence to spit out a mouthful of dirt and then shuffled down the slope past the Green house, her legs bending and catching, her back on fire. At the bottom of the hill she stopped and stood looking at her own house across the water. She couldn't go home; she couldn't face it yet. She would take her punishment in the morning.

There was only one other place to go, and that was Nelson's house. She was just about to pass the stand of trees that would hide her own house from view when her eye was caught by a flickering on the far bank of the creek.

She stopped and turned. She was so tired that her eyes swam in and out of focus, and it took her a few moments to see that the flickering was a small fire half hidden by scrims of vines and bamboo. It burned on the wash of rocks, once a dam, that edged the creek just past her parents' garden. The little area was overgrown with brambles and inelegant young trees, and though the Markos attempted to reclaim it every few years with clippers and shovels, it maintained a life separate from the rest of the yard, a rocky waste sheltering groundhogs and snakes. A light breeze started up, and as Livy brushed her dirty hair out of her eyes she saw her parents.

They were standing by the fire with their heads bowed and their arms crossed. The hair stood up on the back of Livy's neck. They looked very tired, and the breeze was carrying the sharp, piney smell of marijuana.

Livy stared. Her parents were talking across the fire, and the smell was thick in the air, overpowering, almost comical. She put her hands to her face and the open scrape on her cheek stung at her touch. Livy looked over her shoulder, as if expecting to see someone who might corroborate the scene. Her mother sat down on a stone, her elbows on her knees, and pulled her long skirt tight around her legs. Her father stirred the fire pit. A column of sparks went up. They were burning a pile of uprooted pot plants.

She'd seen an IMAX movie as a kid, and when they turned on the lights at the end, the screen was transparent and the wall behind it was a mass of machinery. She was jolted in that way now. Were her parents often in the yard at night? Did they take long walks alone? She was awash in obvious connections. Their anxiety from the beginning of the blockade—their weird, abrupt anger. They had to have been growing it here, on the wash, in the gaps between the rocks.

The argument over her sitting on the chimney clicked into focus. They must have wanted to tear up the plants before the police came to search on the first day of the blockade, but they couldn't while she was sitting up there—she had a perfect view of the whole yard and would have seen them going into the trees. So they had huddled in the house with a bucket full of diluted Clorox, trying to pass the time plausibly until she came down, and when that hadn't worked they'd lost their tempers and ordered her into her room. They'd been out of the house, she remembered, for at least an hour afterward, but she was too annoyed to pay much attention at the time. She'd been stuffing old magazines in a bag while they hopped around on the rocks, pulling up the sticky plants.

It was funny. Christ, it was funny. She sat down on the bank and laughed as quietly as she could, her stomach muscles aching from the effort. They looked so desperately serious. They must have been in a panic all week, trying to figure out how they could hide their crop from the suddenly omnipresent police. Was that the memory from before, as well? The time when, at eight or nine, she had stood with her mother and watched the police cruiser come down the driveway, chewing on the

fingers of one hand and holding on to the pocket of her
mother's skirt with the other, feeling the anxiety radiat-
ing from her like heat from a stove. These pot plants had
been the cause then too. Well, not these, but their ances-
tors. It was just a guess, but it fit.

The Inskys probably got high too. As soon as the
thought occurred to her, it took on the armature of fact:
of course they got high too. All those dinner parties. And
when else did her parents smoke? They took long walks
together on Sunday afternoons—of course. She pictured
them way up at the top of the hill with a bowl and a
book of matches, huddling behind a bush to get out of
the wind. Livy had always hidden her own stash carefully, guessing she would get a long lecture from both
parents and a day or two of silent treatment if it were
found. Her stash was a packet of tinfoil inside an old
music box on a low shelf, the lid decorated with a Gib-
son girl, a knowing profile with a little comma of a chin.

Her mother had once lost patience with the state
of Livy's room and cleaned it while Livy was at school.
Livy remembered her panic when she got home. She
climbed the stairs to her room with her mother's airy
"I straightened up today" echoing in her ears and went
straight for the box. The weed was still there, under a
nest of old necklaces and ribbons. But the lid—she was
almost sure of this now—had been *dusted*.

She and Nelson had always believed that they were good at hiding their smoking. They'd never been caught, after all. Two sets of people squatting in the mud under bridges with jury-rigged pipes. Poking holes in tinfoil for a screen. Both sets thinking they were being enormously clever. Very sneaky! Giggling at each other.

Livy hugged her knees and straightened her back. She felt strangely exhilarated. Just now, from where she sat in this spot, the world seemed to hang together coherently—a trick of perspective, like a jumble of shapes in a mobile that coalesces into an animal at the right angle. The world hung together on a thread of deception, and any deception she could think of seemed equally, mercifully petty. Her own faults, her own betrayals and omissions and the crimes she had recently committed, were blasted apart into undifferentiated bits. She felt very old, but also very light. She stood up again and retreated.

The walk up Collier was punishing on her back and legs. Nelson's house seemed smaller than usual, socketed in the hillside with its two front steps, its protective hedge beside the mailbox. She went around to Nelson's window and scratched on the screen.

Some creature chirped in the dark. It was Tilly, Nelson's cat. She could see her moving, dimly, in the space below the window.

"Goddammit, Nelson," she whispered.

She pushed the sash up a little and the screen toppled. It fell inward, onto the carpet, and the cat chirped again. The door opened across the room and Nelson was there, hurrying toward the window, whispering.

"Jesus, I am so sorry," he said. "She caught me trying to leave. The dog next door started barking and she ran out and got me by the arm." He was leaning out the window. "Janine finally got her to take an Ativan. She just went to sleep."

He pulled Livy over the windowsill, one arm tight around her waist. She gasped at the pressure on her bruised rib. "It's okay," she said, her feet finding the carpet. "I figured something happened."

"I had to sit with her in the living room for an hour and when she finally went to bed it was too late to come meet you." He lit a couple of candles on the dresser. His glasses were on crooked and he had no shirt on. "Are you okay? What happened to your face?"

"I fell," Livy said. She drifted where she stood, as if drunk. The ebbing of the adrenaline in her blood had left her quivery and indistinct.

"Do you want some rubbing alcohol for it?"

"My face? Does it look bad?"

"Yes."

She held up her arm.

"Well, that's worse," he said.

She giggled hoarsely. He went across the hall to the bathroom for alcohol and cotton pads. She sat on the floor, in the corner made by his dresser and bed, and closed her eyes.

"Here," he said, coming back in and taking hold of her wrist. There was something cold on her arm in the semidark and then the burn of the antiseptic. She inhaled through her teeth. "Now your face," he said. He pressed a cotton pad soaked in rubbing alcohol against her scraped cheek, and it stung. His face was very close to hers. She could see the tiny, precise movements of his eyes, the twitches in the skin of his eyelids. "He's gone?" he said.

"I hope so," she said. "He got onto the trail, anyway." It was strange to be so close to someone without making eye contact. It was like they were spying on each other. She could examine him: the corner of his lip, the bristle along his jaw. There were tears in her eyes from the sting of the alcohol.

"I'm really sorry," he said again.

He lifted the cotton pad away from her skin, and then put his arm around her neck and kissed her forehead. She froze. She could feel his breath in her hair. She thought he would regret this in a moment, that he would realize what he was doing and be embarrassed— because it was just her, because he must not mean it—but seconds ticked by and he did not retreat. Cautiously, she hooked her arm around his waist. He was warm, leaning into her, and he was balanced very precisely, his weight on one knee and a hand braced against the side of his bed. Soon he would have to shift either forward or back. Livy tensed her arm across his waist.

He kissed her hair, then her ear. She turned toward him and he kissed her mouth. His thumb was at the hinge of her jaw and his fingers were in her hair.

For a minute they tried to occupy the same space at the same time. They were chest to chest, he was kissing her neck, and she was putting all her strength into closing the circle of her arm around his back. There was a muteness and blindness to this, a faint ridiculousness. Her face was pressed against his bare shoulder.

They slid onto the floor and there was a sharp pain from her rib as he put his weight on her. She coughed. "I fell on a rock," she said.

"I'm sorry," he said. He looked anxious. He pushed himself up onto his hands.

"It's okay." They were staring at each other. She put up her hand and pulled his glasses off, interrupting their eye contact. He looked worried now, as if he had done something wrong. He was in an aggressive position, crouched over her, and he looked suddenly aware of it, and embarrassed. She squeezed his wrist. "Lie next to me?" she said.

He lay on his back. She rolled onto her side and put her arm across his chest.

"Can I sleep here?" she said.

"Yes."

"I just don't want to go home yet."

"Sure. Yes."

She lay with her face close to the side of his neck, and her fatigue compressed her into this tiny space, the cove of his shoulder, the dusty carpet under her head.

She woke up a little while later and he was kneeling, tugging on her arm. "You should get into bed," he said.

The bed was barely wide enough for both of them. They kissed again. She bit his shoulder experimentally; it was salty. He pushed her shirt up to her armpits. His hands were warm and dry but when he put his mouth on her breast she stiffened. "Stop," she said. He was moving differently, there was something frenzied and impersonal about it, and if he saw too much of her he would forget that they were friends. He pulled her shirt back down and put his arms around her waist.

✳

She woke up several times during the night and lay quietly, trying to flex her legs without waking him up. She thought of her parents standing by the fire. She hoped they were finished burning it, and it was safely buried and they were in bed, and that the police would have no reason to pick their way into the wash. Nelson murmured in his sleep.

People she knew at school were always getting the idea of growing their own, and they were always being found out by their parents, or their neighbors, or their younger siblings toddling into the hedges and coming back with handfuls of it. It was an indiscreet plant. It had that prickly, caustic smell. She knew from a couple of boys she worked with at the restaurant that growing it was complicated and time-consuming, and it took the single-mindedness of a person in love with the plant. She thought of her parents going for walks together in the afternoons on her mother's days off. Livy had always been happy to stay in the house and watch TV while they were gone. It was nice to flip through the channels without their disapproval, moral or aesthetic, hovering in the background through the kitchen door. If she'd been more in the habit of going outside during those intervals she probably would have spotted them a hundred feet from the house, barely hidden in the woods.

Her parents had always been uncomfortable in groups, at children's birthday parties, at Girl Scout jamborees, at Parents' Night. There was an air always coming from them—Livy was just now identifying it—that they expected to be disapproved of, and took some pride in it. She knew people like that at school, too. It was a little childish, this ostentatious claiming of separateness, and so was the large risk they were taking for the small pleasure of getting high and the little bit of money that must come from selling to the neighbors. She felt like a traitor in some way for calling them childish. But it was true. At the same time, she felt a new, sharp imperative to protect them. To keep away trouble like Revaz and Dominic, and the police.

She rolled over and her knees collided with Nelson's. He murmured something. She couldn't tell if he was awake or not. She turned her back to him and he shifted easily into the space she made: his belly to her back, his bent knees to her bent knees.

4

When Revaz had been riding for forty-five minutes he risked a stop at an all-night gas station. There were only two other people inside, both men, and they looked just as haggard as he did, just as sluggish, blinking in the same suspect manner in the bright light. There were road maps in a stand by the door. He took one, then went to the counter and pointed to the rack behind the clerk, where hot dogs turned on rollers under a red lamp.

He ate the hot dog in the dark behind the building, where he had left the bicycle. When it was gone he stood there hesitating for several minutes and then went back in and bought another one. The clerk smiled when he handed him the change, nodded to the hot dog, then pointed at his own face, and Revaz realized he had mustard on his chin.

The moon had dipped below the trees, and it was quite dark outside. He stood beside the pumps, slowly eating the last of the hot dog, tracing out his route in the light of the filling canopy. Another forty-five minutes on the bike and he would be at the train. His stomach was full, and the night was cool. Insects shrieked and thrummed in the trees that edged the lot—sounds of the forest barely held at bay by the highway. The asphalt crumbled at the edges, turning to burr-filled weeds. It seemed entirely plausible, for a minute, that he could run and keep running forever. Pleasant, even. He climbed onto the bike.

※

When Livy opened her eyes the room was starting to lighten, gray now instead of black. Nelson had rolled away and was lying with his back to her, one shoulder humped high, the sheet pressed tight under his arm. The weak early light was like a resin that filled the room, fixing the objects in it. During the school year she woke at this time of day but had to get up and dress quickly, and it was rare for her to be still in this stillness. Revaz was far away by now, long gone. Her part was done. Nelson moved beside her.

"How are you?" he said. His eyes were bright from sleep. He propped himself on an elbow and rubbed his face.

"Fine," she said. She noticed she had pulled the sheet up so that only her head and neck were showing over the top of it. It was one thing to go to sleep next to a friend, and another to wake up there. "How are you?" she said.

"Fine." He put his arms around her and squeezed her hard, pressed his face against her neck. The bruises on her hip ached. The embrace seemed to press her spine straight, ease out the kinks caused by a night in a narrow space. He had broad, flat hands.

"I don't want to go home yet," she said.

"You definitely shouldn't."

She laughed. They were lying very close together, which meant they didn't have to look each other in the eye. His hands moved over her stomach in a friendly way, as if brushing crumbs off it.

"My parents are going to be worried," she said.

"It's probably not even six yet. They're asleep." He touched the scrape on her cheek. "This scabbed over pretty well."

"What am I going to tell people?" She put her fingers to her cheek. It was hard to the touch.

"That you fell."

"I've been saying I fell a lot lately. I told my dad I flipped my bike over in some gravel and that was why I had these scratches . . ." She indicated her arms. "I wonder when they'll notice the bike is gone. My mom hasn't used it in years." She bit her lip. "Maybe they'll just think somebody stole it. They don't lock the garage."

Nelson put his arm across her chest. She took a long, tired breath. "I don't really see a way we can get out of all this with everything together," she said.

He lifted his head off the pillow and looked at her for a minute. She was tempted at first to look away; he was shirtless, one bare arm was across her chest, and this was a position familiar mostly from movies—male propped up thoughtfully on one elbow, female on her back. The intimacy between them was ordinary and alien at the same time. She made herself look him in the eye. He put one hand flat across her face, covering her left eye and the scrape on her cheek, and kissed her forehead. He lay back down. He wasn't going to say anything, she thought, because he agreed with her.

"I wonder if your mom's awake," she said.

"Probably not."

Livy sat up. "I'm hungry," she said. "I'm *so* hungry."

Nelson lit up. "We should open the blizzard box."

"There's still a blizzard box?"

The blizzard box was a metal locker in the garage filled with canned and freeze-dried food, in case of a major snowstorm. Nelson's mother was prepared for all kinds of emergencies. Nelson had grown up practicing house-evacuation drills twice a year, when the clocks were set forward and back; waking up to shrieking tests of the fire, radon, and carbon monoxide detectors; memorizing rendezvous points in the neighborhood, the county, the state. The blizzard box was always stocked but never touched.

They climbed out of bed. Livy's hunger rolled through her, pitching and reeling. They crept down the dark carpeted hallway, their breathing light and shallow, and Nelson heaved open the door from the kitchen to the garage. Livy saw the locker half hidden under a plastic toboggan and dragged it out into the light. They sat cross-legged on the floor beside it.

"Beans, corn, blueberries, pumpkin, condensed milk, condensed milk, condensed milk," she said, pulling out the cans.

"Beans and corn," Nelson said. "If we had tortillas . . ."

"Tomato soup, mandarin oranges, pearl onions, olives, minestrone soup," she said.

His brownish knee was bent beside hers. "I love mandarin oranges."

"Look at all this condensed milk. Let's make pudding."

"Taco salad and pudding."

They carried armloads back into the house. His mother would be furious, but they would be full of pudding and it wouldn't matter that much. Nelson turned the radio on the counter on.

"Are you sure?" Livy said.

"She's a really heavy sleeper after an Ativan," he said.

Janine appeared in the doorway, trailing a sheet. "Is that Mom's hurricane stash?"

"Yeah," Nelson said.

"You're asking to get killed," she said, and shuffled back into the dark of the living room.

They were too hungry to wait for the food to heat. They ate the beans and corn with spoons, cold. Livy dipped her fingers in sweetened condensed milk and licked it off, over and over. Nelson made a stack of empty mandarin orange cans. The radio swooned in the corner.

"These are so good," Livy said, studying a spoonful of beans. "Better than normal, for beans." The window over the sink faced east and the sun was just coming up over the hill. The woods were a dark, cool mass. She could look straight out at the horizon from the kitchen. She stood at the sink with her spoon, eating one bean at a time, watching the sun rise. Nelson stood beside her.

"The Harbor County standoff enters its fifth day," said the radio.

They both lurched toward the volume knob.

"Federal law enforcement officers seeking the arrest of a foreign national have been at an impasse outside Maronne since Monday morning, after tracking him there on Sunday." It was a woman's voice, maybe from one of the Philadelphia stations, or a national one. "Revaz Deni is under an extradition order from the Republic of Georgia. At a press conference on Tuesday a spokesman for the Federal Bureau of Investigation was reluctant to reveal further details, citing security concerns and an ongoing investigation by international partners."

"Georgia?" Livy said.

"Nearby Maronne is growing tense as the standoff drags on," the woman said. "Some expressed anger at the way police are handling the situation." An old man spoke against a background of tinny traffic noise. "It's been a mess," he said. "Everybody thinks so."

"We'll bring you updates as we receive them," the woman said.

The traffic report started up. Nelson turned it off.

"Georgia?" Livy said. "Where is that? It's under Russia, isn't it?"

"I think so. It's not in the Balkans, anyway," Nelson said.

"I don't know anything about Georgia."

"I wish I still had that encyclopedia."

"The *Kid's World Book*?" Livy laughed. The book had a cracked spine and had been kept in the bathroom, and she had leafed through it idly so many times that she had memorized the format of its brightly illustrated pages. "If only. We could look up their annual rainfall."

"Well, it would be something," Nelson said.

"Knowing doesn't help now anyway," Livy said.

The kitchen was the brightest room in the house. Livy wanted it to be very early in the morning forever. It was the best, most private time of day, and the air was cool. It was easy to believe that she and Nelson were the only people awake for miles. They ate until they were full and rinsed the cans out in the sink. They were drinking instant coffee with powdered creamer at the kitchen table, sitting in two chairs pulled close together in a pool of light, when there was knocking at the door. Livy's stomach turned over. She saw an instant of panic on Nelson's face before he caught his breath.

"I'll get it," he said.

They could hear Janine shifting on the sofa in the dark living room. "Somebody's knocking," she called.

"I *know*, J," Nelson said.

Livy got up and followed him. There was an obscure protective impulse in this. She jogged across the living room in his wake, plucking at the borrowed shirt so it billowed away from her chest. She saw him catch his breath and then jerk open the door.

Ron Cash was standing there, the top of his bald head shiny as glass.

"Good morning," he said.

"Oh, thank God." Livy stopped and covered her face briefly with her hands. She had meant *Thank God it's not the cops*, and had come close to saying it out loud. Janine sat up, blinking in the light from the doorway. All the shades were down and she looked annoyed at the intrusion. "You shouldn't bang on the *door* like that," she said.

"We're doing a search," Ron said. His hands were folded in front of him, over his belt buckle. There were other people with him, though Livy couldn't see yet who they were; she heard low voices, and the clear morning light through the doorway was interrupted by a jumble of shadows.

"You're looking for the guy?" Nelson said.

"That's correct," Ron said. Livy tensed. She thought Nelson might glance at her at this mention of Revaz, and that people would notice, but he didn't turn. He stepped aside and pushed open the door with a little shrug. Livy saw, in the clump of people now stepping up from the grass to the concrete steps, the bobbing ponytail and long anxious face of Jocelyn.

Jocelyn saw her too. "Your parents are looking for you," she said.

"I know," Livy said. She backed away.

"My parents are sleeping," Nelson said in Ron's direction.

The small living room was suddenly full. Jocelyn walked into the kitchen and Livy heard the pantry door open and shut. Ron and a couple of men from the sprawling Christmas household on White Horse Road went single file down the narrow hallway, toward the back of the house. They all seemed too big for the place. Ron stopped at the end of the hall and knocked on the door of the master bedroom with the back of his hand.

"Tom," he called. "Tom, Sarah. Sorry to disturb you."

"Your parents are going to know I'm here," Livy whispered. Nelson looked alarmed. The bedroom door opened and they heard a suggestion of Mrs. Tela's voice.

"Let's wait in the garage," Nelson said.

They found Lena Spellar out there. She was standing under the high, shallow arch of the automatic garage door, drawing from an electronic cigarette, her free arm braced across her stomach. She smiled. There was a diffuse kind of regret in the smile, something less personal than an apology.

"Hi, kids," she said.

"You're here with them?" Livy said.

Lena shrugged. "I haven't been sleeping well."

Livy looked down at the ransacked blizzard box. "Where's Dominic?" she said. She had to clear her throat.

"At home."

Livy glanced at Nelson. He was looking out at the yard, not reacting, and she was grateful again for his coolness.

"Has Ron already been to your place?" Livy said. She tried to make the question sound neutral, although she was starting to think it didn't matter, that no one paid any attention to her anyway.

"Not yet," Lena said. "We started at the top of the hill."

Livy thought, *I want to go up on somebody's roof and just let the wind blow over me and not have to come down.* "I'm going to go home," she said. She turned to Nelson. "Come with me."

Nelson looked surprised. "Okay."

Livy walked out onto the driveway and kept going, up the little curve to the road. She was barefoot. Nelson caught up with her by the mailbox.

"Are we going to Dominic's?" he said. "We should have put shoes on." He looked down at his feet, hurrying along after her on the fine gravel.

"Yeah," Livy said. "We can at least warn him." So that he could do what? Turn Mark loose? As if the pharmaceutical assistant were a cornered mouse they could shoo out into the yard. Would the police recognize him, if they saw him? It was possible that he was already a famous victim on the other side of the roadblocks, his picture circulating on the news, all that. Although they had not heard anything on the radio. She fought the urge to break into a run. Anyone looking out an east-facing window, anywhere on Collier, could see her and Nelson hurrying toward the low road.

"Where do you think he is now?" Nelson said.

"Mark?" she said.

"Your guy."

"He's not mine. He's in Cooverton, I hope to God. How long does it take to bike twelve miles?"

"An hour, more if he's slow."

There was plywood over the inside of Jocelyn's door. They hurried down the final slope to the little row of houses beside the Sportsmen's Club. Livy was holding Nelson's hand. They ran up the Spellar steps and banged on the door and then pushed through it without waiting. No one was in the living room.

"Dominic!" she yelled. "It's Livy!"

"What!" Dominic called from upstairs.

They ran up. Dominic opened his bedroom door. Mark was asleep on the sleeping bag, his head on the floor beside the pillow. Brian was sitting in a desk chair, spinning slowly in place.

"People are coming," Livy said.

Nelson dropped to his knees beside Mark. "Hey, wake up," he said.

"Who's coming?" said Dominic.

"Your mom and Ron Cash and a bunch of other people. They're searching all the houses." She was out of breath. Nelson was shaking Mark gently, and it was making his head bobble back and forth.

"Dom, is he still on pills?" Livy said.

"Muscle relaxers."

"What are you *doing* to him?" she said.

"I keep *asking* him and he keeps saying yes!"

Mark's eyes were fluttering open. He fixed them on Nelson. His eyebrows went up very slowly.

"Hi, Mark," Nelson said. "Are you okay?"

"Dom?" Mark said.

"I'm right here, man," Dominic said. He took a glass pipe out of his top drawer.

"This is not a good time to smoke, Dom," Livy said. He ignored her.

"Where can we hide him?" Nelson said.

"Basement?" Dominic said. He shrugged. "Backyard?"

"I think they're going to look in those places, Dom," Nelson said.

"There's no super-secret place?" Livy said. "No place not obvious?"

Dominic shook his head. He was crumbling a bud between his fingers. "Not really."

"You don't seem worried," she said.

"Well, you do." He looked at her. "Is it helping?"

Nelson had one arm around Mark's back and was trying to get him to sit up. Mark wore an expression of confusion that made Livy's chest ache like it was packed in ice. He seemed to be having trouble focusing his eyes, holding his head up; he was like a baby. He cleared his throat. "This room," he said.

"I'm so sorry this happened," Livy said.

He squinted at her. There were bits of sleeping bag lint on his buzzed hair. "I don't know who you are," he said.

"We can leave or we can stay here," Dominic said. "It doesn't make a difference."

Mark was rubbing his face with one hand, absent-mindedly pushing down a morning hard-on with the other. Nelson pretended to study the leaves at the window.

"What do we say when they get here?" Livy said.

"I'll tell them what happened," Dominic said. His lighter wasn't working. He frowned at it.

"What'll that be?" she said. "Tell me what you'll say."

"It's okay, Livy," Nelson said.

"I'm checking," she said.

"I'll say we went to the pharmacy," Dominic said. "And I took Mark."

"And you were the one with the gun," Livy said.

"Yeah, obviously," Dominic said. "That's what happened."

She hadn't known him well before the blockade. They said hello in school, she saw him sometimes when she was coming and going from work. She watched him take a long hit from the glass piece. She was angry at him for the way things had gone, this whole mess he had made, his dickish bravado, his stupid gun. Sunk under the anger was a deep and terrible pity. "You're still seventeen, aren't you?" she said. "If the police find out, it won't be so bad, maybe."

"I'm sixteen."

"You are? We're the same age?" He was so tall. His hands were so big, the pipe and lighter lost in them.

He didn't look up. "Yeah."

Mark was sitting up under his own power now, slumped over folded legs, looking perturbed. His lower lip stuck out. "I'm thirsty," he said.

"I'll get water," Nelson said. He left the room.

"You want some of this?" Dominic said. He held the piece out to Livy.

"No, thanks." She went out and sat at the top of the carpeted stairs. Nelson came up, one hand on the banister, holding a big plastic cup of water with a football helmet on the side.

"This feels like hide-and-seek," she said. "When you're really bad at it." He laughed. "I'm serious," she said. The staircase was dim and her own eyes felt enormously wide. "I was always terrible at it and I remember what it felt like. It felt like this."

"It'll probably be twenty minutes before they get here," Nelson said, putting his hand over hers. "Half an hour." It was always hard to tell when he was afraid. His face was more opaque than hers, less mobile, his eyes deep-set and dark behind his glasses.

Mark pushed open the door from Dominic's room suddenly and stopped in the doorway, backlit, in a T-shirt and boxer shorts.

"People are coming for me?" he said.

Nelson offered him the water. He drank half of it without stopping to breathe and then wiped his chin on his arm. "I should probably go home," he said to Nelson, his eyebrows creeping up. "My sister is going to be *pissed*."

Nelson tried an encouraging expression. "Okay," he said.

"Let's wait downstairs," Livy said. "I'm sick of sitting in the dark."

They sat in the living room, all four of them, lined up on a green sofa in front of the dead television. The window behind the TV was curtained with white pointelle; a spider plant climbed a couple of bamboo sticks in a pot. Lena Spellar had nice things, Livy thought. She hadn't noticed it before. The room was all white and green.

Brian lit a cigarette, got up and retrieved a ceramic ashtray from the kitchen, and sat back down on the sofa. For a long time no one spoke.

"What's on TV at seven in the morning?" Livy said finally.

"Cartoons," said Dominic.

"Oh, right," Livy said. "Of course." When she was a child she'd woken at seven every morning, without the aid of an alarm clock, and watched cartoons in the shadowed living room with the volume turned so low she had to sit within arm's reach of the screen. She thought of little children doing that all over Harbor County that morning, at that very hour. The thought of their concentrating faces quieted her mind. She lived in an emergency that covered only a handful of addresses. She stroked the inside of Nelson's wrist with the tips of her fingers.

They heard voices outside, and then saw moving shadows on the curtains. The group of searchers didn't knock; Lena was with them, and she just pushed the front door open and stood aside. Ron was behind her, looking in all directions. Lena stared at the sofa.

"What are you all doing here?" she said.

There was a beat of perhaps two seconds after that, a suspended interval. Then Lena said, "Who are you?"

Mark didn't seem to realize she was talking to him. He looked at Livy and Nelson, then Dominic.

"Who's he?" Ron said, jutting through the doorway. Jocelyn crowded in behind them, along with Maurice Carden.

"Him? Is that him?" Jocelyn said. She pointed at Mark from the doorway, her eyes alight. "We found him?"

"He's too young," Lena said.

"No he's not, he looks like him," Jocelyn said. Her face was strange, the eyes round, an expression of delight half forming, then fading, then forming again around her mouth. "His hair is all buzzed off, that's why he looks different from the picture."

"No, we took him from the Quick Drug," Dominic said.

"That's him," Jocelyn said. "That's his face."

"He shouldn't be here," Ron said.

Lena said, "That's not him. Dom, where did he come from?"

"My room."

"He shouldn't *be* here," Jocelyn said.

"Who the hell are you?" Ron said, coming close. The four on the sofa all seemed to be frozen, staring up at him.

"Open your mouth," Jocelyn said to Mark. "Say something. You speak English?"

"He speaks English, he's from Riverview!" Dominic said. He stood up. The ashtray fell off the arm of the sofa, a soft thump on the carpet.

"Why'd they say he was foreign, then?" Ron said. He looked pained. His teeth were gritted. "Why have they been *lying* to us?"

"No, no, no, no," Livy said. She was half out of her seat.

"What's your name, sweetheart?" said Lena.

"Mark," said Mark.

Ron took hold of his arm and pulled him up off the sofa. "We're getting him out of here," he said.

"Take him to the cops," Jocelyn said.

"Riverview?" Lena said. Then: "He's just a kid."

Ron pulled Mark out the door. Livy was buffeted by the sudden space on the sofa, like a plastic bag caught in the backdraft of a car. She got up too and followed them onto the porch. "It's not him!" she shouted, but Ron wasn't listening, pulling Mark ahead and into the street.

"Where's Ron taking him?" Lena said.

"To the cops," Dominic said, his hands pressed to his head.

Livy ran after them. Jerry Olds was standing barefoot in his yard across the road, the cuffs of his pants rolled up, a pale shirt unbuttoned to his chest. The rest of Ron's search party, a few dozen people from the houses that had already been searched, were arrayed around the intersection, looking down toward them with interest. Ron and Mark pushed through the little crowd with Jocelyn right behind them.

"Ron, wait!" Dominic yelled. "Wait, wait, wait!" The people at the intersection seemed to sense that something exciting had happened, and they moved uncertainly toward the bridge. Clarence and Aurelia Green stood on the front steps of the store. Livy saw them as she ran past, her feet raw against the ground, her breath suddenly burning in her throat.

"Livy, you have to go home," Clarence called to her. "You're killing your mom and dad, they've been all over looking for you."

Livy had lost sight of Mark. She tried to weave through the crowd, her hands balled up into fists. Nelson was a few paces behind, Dominic up ahead. She passed the straggle of houses on Prospect, rounded the curve in the road where the earth dropped off steeply to the water, and came out into the open. Ron was holding Mark by the elbow and Jocelyn was waving her arms beside them, her hair falling loose around her thin face. Dominic limped after them, trying to catch up: there was real pain in his face now, his foot must have been getting worse for days. Two policemen in powder-blue Maronne PD uniforms flanked the van on the other side of the barricade.

"We have your guy!" Jocelyn called to them.

"You don't!" Dominic yelled. "You're wrong!"

One of the policemen spoke into the radio on his shoulder. "Don't come any closer!" shouted the other.

"Here he is!" Ron said, pushing Mark forward. Mark stumbled a few feet and turned his head slowly this way and that, squinting at Ron, taking a long stiff-shouldered look at the police by the van. "Go on," Ron said, shoving him again.

The crowd was growing. People were coming out of the houses on Forgeman's Row, drawn by the noise through open windows, and clumping together with the members of Ron's search party. Thirty or forty people now stood in the road, craning their necks. Ron gave Mark one more push and the boy started to walk toward the barricade, head down, trailing untied laces. The shouting started again from the cops, the raised hands. "Stop right there!"

Mark's eyes were half-closed. He was still high on muscle relaxers, and he walked as if a string connected to his navel were pulling him forward, tilted at the hips with his arms and legs loose, squinting in the sun that cut at a low angle down the road. Dominic went after him, adding his rumbling voice to the chorus of yells. "Mark, stop! Stop!" he said, out in front now and alone, reaching after him. Mark stopped without looking back, sat down on the ground and crossed his legs slowly, laboriously, moving his knees with his hands. The back of his white shirt was soaked through with sweat. He bowed his head. Dominic reached him and tugged on his arms.

"Dominic, come back here right *now*," Lena shouted. Nelson made a move to go after him, but Livy grabbed his arm: the policemen had both unholstered their guns.

More vans appeared from the highway, taking the left onto Prospect Road too hard.

Ron waved his hands at Mark's back. "Go *on*, I said!" He looked back at the crowd, appealing to them, showing them his palms. "Get him out of here!" he shouted. His voice was so hoarse it had no pitch. "Get it over with!" he cried.

Dominic had gotten Mark to his feet and was walking him back toward the crowd, holding him up, the skinny boy sagging against his broad chest. "Don't bring him back here!" Ron yelled, his voice cracking as it went higher. He was holding a pistol. He lifted it—it shone briefly. He stepped toward Mark, seizing his arm.

There were panicked shouts and then a pop that perforated the air. Ron stopped percussively, one knee lifted, his chin abruptly pressing toward his chest, and then he was a heap on the ground and blood was everywhere. There was a sigh from the crowd, a terrible sound Livy had never heard before, the air draining from so many lungs. The policemen toppled the sawhorses and ran toward them, one shouting into his radio, the other with his gun still drawn. A wave of people pushed forward, toward Ron where he lay on the ground, and at the same time another wave pushed backward, as half the crowd began to flee toward the bridge. It was at that moment that another bang, like a gun but not quite like a gun, sounded from up the road. A couple of silver canisters ricocheted off the retaining wall that held back the hill and skittered across the asphalt. Livy turned in confu sion to Nelson. She had a moment to notice the panic on his face before a cloud of tear gas hit her.

She was momentarily blinded and suffocated. She tried to run, her knees banging together, her eyes squeezed shut. "Nelson! Nelson! Nelson!" she shrieked. She forced her eyes open and saw the wheeling dark hill and the white glare of the sky and then closed them again. She dropped to her hands and knees, coughing, and someone collided with her, fell over her back and lay beside her retching. She put out a hand and found an elbow.

"Dom?" she said.

Someone was shouting, "Fuck." There were running feet. She turned toward the roadblock and opened her eyes: red and blue lights. The elbow pulled away. It was Dominic, she could hear him muttering to himself.

"We gotta get up," she said.

Nelson was on the other side of her. She got to her feet, tears running down her cheeks. Her vision was pale and mottled, as if haphazardly bleached. Policemen were dragging the roadblock aside, and more were pouring out of a van just coming to a stop. Dominic pushed him- self up and ran. Livy and Nelson went after him, back the way they had come. At the intersection of White Horse and Prospect Livy spun to look back, tripped over her own feet, and toppled backward, hitting her head.

There was a warm darkness. When she opened her eyes Nelson was crouched over her, his glasses missing. The police were a hum in the air, a change in color. She knew they were everywhere but could not keep her eyes open to see them. Someone was chanting—many people were chanting—voices shouting "On the ground" over and over, with an interspersed chorus of weird sputtering and wailing and cursing that seemed to respond but not connect, as if she were hearing the soundtracks to two movies playing over each other. She pushed herself up on one elbow and put her head on Nelson's leg. She could hear a woman sobbing nearby. "Who's crying?" she said.

"Ron's wife," he said. He kneaded her arm with his fingers.

"They shot him," she said, unnecessarily. "Can you see?"

"Not really."

Her own eyes were shut. It hurt less that way. She felt the collar of his T-shirt with one hand and then put her face against it. The burning in her eyes made it hard for her to control her balance. Ron Cash's wife was crying and cursing.

"What's happening?" Livy said.

"They're arresting everybody."

She lifted her face away from his shirt and narrowed her eyes at the road. There were streaks in her vision. It was like old glass and the sunlight burned and burned. She saw Dominic sitting against the bridge wall and little Lena Spellar with her arms around him, balanced on the balls of her feet.

"Where's Mark?" she said.

"I don't know," Nelson said. He sounded sad.

She closed her eyes and counted to ten and then opened them again, wiping tears and mucus off her face. There was Jocelyn, in her red shirt, with a policeman in a navy blue uniform pulling both her hands behind her back. Jocelyn was shaking her head like an animal, her hair sweeping her shoulders. There was a burned smell everywhere. Livy thought of running, but she could barely stand and there was nowhere for the two of them to go.

She was seized by the wrists and pulled upward. She smelled sweat and floral deodorant; cuffs clicked on her wrists. "Get down," said a woman's voice. Livy's knees were pushed out from under her and she was down again, her cheek pressed against the road. Knuckly hands pressed all over her body, into her armpits, under her stomach, high up between her legs.

"She's clean," said a woman.

Nelson caught his breath beside her. A policeman was pressing his foot down between Nelson's shoulder blades, leaning on him, while the woman patted him down. Livy went rigid. The scab on her cheek had torn open and there was blood in her mouth. The policeman stepped away from Nelson and crouched in front of her.

"What happened to your face?" he said.

She looked at Nelson and then understood that this was the wrong thing to do. "Nothing," she said. She had to lift her head to speak clearly. "I fell."

"You fell? On your face?"

The man had a chip in one of his front teeth. She stared at it.

"Is that what happened to your arms, too?" he said.

She couldn't see them but she could feel the raw places. There was the wide scrape along her forearm, and the earlier scratches too, from running through the woods when they came back from the pharmacy. "I fell out of a tree," she said. Saliva ran over her lip. She couldn't wipe her mouth.

"Is that right? You climb trees?"

"Yes sir."

"Fucked yourself up pretty bad."

"Yes sir." Something more was needed. He was staring at her, his blond eyebrows beetling. "It was stupid," she said.

He leaned down close to Nelson. "Are you a friend of hers?"

"Yes," he said.

"Is that what happened to her? She fell out of a tree?"

"Yes."

"She's clumsy like that? She climbs trees, gets banged up?"

"Yes, sir, she does that a lot."

"She seems a little old to be climbing trees."

Nelson breathed deeply once or twice. He was trying to collect himself. "You're never too old," he said.

The policeman raised his eyebrows. "You're full of shit," he said, but then he laughed.

"Call an ambulance, ambulance, ambulance, ambulance," cried Ron Cash's wife. Her voice seemed to come to them through the trees. It was the worst kind of scream: an adult scream that whipsawed like a child's. Livy wanted to move across the six inches of gravel that separated her from Nelson.

She saw Jocelyn's shoes and lifted her head. Jocelyn's hair hung over her face. The cop holding her shoulder told her to sit and she hesitated, and then bent at the knees and sat. The three officers stepped to one side and conferred. Jocelyn lifted her head and looked at Livy. Her eyes were bloodshot and her mouth was tightly closed. It was so hot, even in the shadows of the trees, and the sound of the creek at the bottom of the hill made Livy thirsty.

"Did you see Mark?" Livy said.

"Who's Mark?" Jocelyn said.

"The kid." Livy shook her head in frustration. "The one you took to the cops."

"You all were hiding him," Jocelyn said. "You stupid whore."

Livy's mouth dropped open. "He's not the one they were looking for." Jocelyn had known her since she was a child. She'd stopped her from crossing the road once when a car was coming.

"You were hiding him!" Jocelyn said. Her face was hollow, her hair sticking to her cheeks.

"Shut up, both of you," said the female officer.

"We didn't want to hurt anybody," Livy said. She started to cry. She pressed her face into the gravel. Shelly Cash had gone quiet. There were sirens in the distance, on the highway, coming closer.

"Why did you do it?" Jocelyn said. "Why did you do it?"

"She didn't do it, you bitch!" Nelson said. "You're *confused*!"

"If you all don't shut the fuck up I'm putting you in the van now," said the policewoman. She spoke into her shoulder. "Carter, how long are we going to wait on that second van?"

Jocelyn was crying. "I want to see my son. I haven't done anything," she said.

A van rumbled around the corner, and then another. Livy was pulled to her feet and her knees failed to lock under her; she felt like she was on skates. Doors slid open. A catbird was screaming close by. She closed her eyes, trying to take the edge off the burning, and when she opened them again she saw several policemen with managerial expressions, hands stretched out in her direction.

They put her in the van with Jocelyn and stone-faced Lena and the grieving Shelly Cash, whose sobbing was hypnotic, a weighted spiral that lifted and dropped. With her eyes closed Livy felt only half-conscious. She was locked in a small space with a handful of pained women and she would never see Nelson again and her parents would never find her. She would live here; it was her world. Ron Cash was everywhere, a shadow on shadows.

5

They were taken to the police station in Maronne. Half-way there the van stopped at a light and Livy pressed her forehead against the wire over the window and looked out. She could see a hatchback waiting patiently beside them at the light, a toddler in a baby seat in the back.

They pulled into the lot behind the police station, bumping a little over the curb. Later Livy remembered this interval as if there had been cotton stuffed in her ears; the bright afternoon was muted. The driver of the van got out and walked around to open the rear door, all business now, not really looking at their faces as he flooded them with light. Livy was stiff and her eyes still burned, but it was bearable now.

The police station was cool, bluish, and bright, like an aquarium. It felt like a long time since she'd been under electric lights. The handful of police at the desks scattered around the room looked up when the little group came in. Shelly Cash had stopped wailing; Livy looked at her and saw that tears were dripping from her chin. It was a mistake to look at this woman, Livy decided. It made her stomach heave. She kept her eyes ahead.

They were led down a narrow tiled hallway. The cop removed their handcuffs and waved them into a holding cell. Livy drifted as far as the back wall and then stopped to turn and look back, like a lap swimmer. It was only then that she noticed Shelly Cash was gone.

Livy sat in the cell with Lena and Jocelyn for hours. From her bench against the wall she could see the narrow gray-and-white hallway and two and a half of the panel lights that lit it. In the distance, she heard shouting and doors clanging open and shut. She and Lena and Jocelyn did not speak or look at each other for a long time. She supposed the two women were thinking of their sons.

Whenever Livy closed her eyes she saw Ron Cash, the laundry-bag heft and shape of him on the ground. She wanted her parents now; their disappointment in her no longer seemed important. She was afraid for them. She hoped they had burned everything, buried the ash. As the time passed her hopes were phrased more and more like prayers. *Please, please, let them be waiting at home.* And every time she closed her eyes: Ron Cash.

✳

At some point Jocelyn said, "They have to let me make a phone call."

Lena said, "Stop."

"They have to."

"They don't have to do shit, Jocelyn."

There was a pause. Livy turned her head slightly to watch them. She was sitting on the bench with her feet drawn up, her back to the corner.

"I didn't do anything," Jocelyn said, "and they can't just leave me here all day. They need to come in here and tell me what they think I did."

"You didn't do anything?" Lena sat up suddenly, straightened her back. "You didn't *do* anything?"

"You want to blame somebody? Look at her." Jocelyn pointed at Livy. "Her and your son, hiding with that guy in your house."

"Stop it," Lena said. "No more talking."

"Who *did* this?" Jocelyn said.

"Your son is safe and I don't know where mine is now," Lena said, "so shut your mouth."

Both women subsided. Livy closed her eyes again. She fell into a light, nauseous sleep on the narrow bench. When she opened her eyes again her parents were standing in the narrow hallway outside the holding cell and a policeman was rolling back the door. She started to cry. Her mother crossed the room and embraced her. The fabric of her dress was rough against Livy's face, seeded with small buttons. Livy held on.

"Why would you get mixed up in something like that?" her mother said. "You see a crowd like that, you run the other way, you understand?"

"I'm sorry," Livy said. She allowed herself to be shaken and rocked. No one knew about the pharmacy, still. She wondered how long it could be.

At the desk they were given release papers; Livy gathered them in numb fingers, held them against her chest. The policeman at the desk was carefully uninterested in them. Each of her parents kept a hand on her as they walked out. It was still daylight outside, a thick, late, honeyed light, and the parking lot was fringed with reporters. A row of irritated policemen patrolled the perimeter, and the camera crews stood just out of their reach, all along the sidewalks and into the street, on the patchy soccer field in the little park across the way, on the front steps of the old YWCA building on the corner. Her parents pulled her toward the car. Neither of them looked her in the face, even while they held on to her. Her mother had been crying.

"Is Ron okay?" Livy said. She knew he was not.

"I don't know," her father said.

She started to cry. She sat in the back seat. She put her seat belt on.

"Where's Nelson?" she said. No one answered her.

They eased out of the parking lot. The police made way. The camera crews pressed closer, then retreated. There was the Laundromat, the red-doored church, the tax preparer, the two Mexican groceries, the Quick Drug. And then they were back on Prospect, approaching the barricade.

"They opened it," Livy said.

The sawhorses and chains were gone, but now there was yellow crime scene tape zigzagging through the deep shadows. A half-dozen squad cars, some of them with their lights silently flashing, were lined up just around the turn. The police stood in small groups, talking, or wandered back and forth among the vehicles. Two uniformed men were leaning against an FBI truck, paper from deli sandwiches spread out on the hood.

"Shit," her father said. "We should have gone back the way we came."

"It's open," Livy said again. "It's over?"

A policeman knocked on her father's window. "Detour. Where are you trying to go?"

"Over the bridge. We live here."

Livy was craning her neck from the back seat, trying to see what the policemen were clustered over in the middle of the road. She thought she could see a bloodstain on the pavement. She closed her eyes, feeling sick again.

"You're going to want to go around by White Horse Road," said the officer.

They drove down White Horse Road and were waved through. As they passed the store they saw the Telas on the steps, Mr. and Mrs. Tela and Janine sitting there with the sun in their eyes. There was no one else in sight: no Nelson, no Noreen sitting on the shaded porch of the house next door, no children with dripping Popsicles along the railing. They looked like the only people left in the world. Livy's father slowed down and Mrs. Tela stood.

"Did you see Nelson?" she called. "Livy? Is that you?" She crossed the intersection and, incredibly, put the palms of her hands flat onto Livy's window. Livy was so disoriented by this weird assault on her parents' car that it took her a moment to roll down the window.

"He's at the station and they won't let me talk to him," Mrs. Tela said.

"I haven't seen him," Livy said. She was relieved at least to know where he was.

Janine padded up behind her mother on bare feet. "They found the guy's hiding spot up in the woods," she said. "They think he left a couple of days ago. They're leaving."

"They screwed this up so bad," Mrs. Tela said.

Livy blinked very slowly. She kept her face still. In the woods? Her mother leaned toward the driver's-side window, her forehead wrinkling. "You're shitting me," she said. "He *was* here? Where?"

Janine nodded. "In a deer blind up at the top of the hill, behind Paula's house."

No one was looking at Livy. She tried to control her face. He must have been hiding in the deer blind before he came to her yard that night. Had he left anything behind in the garage, any sign he'd been there? She would go and check when she got home, if her parents ever let her leave her bedroom.

"Unbelievable," her mother said. "I never really thought it could be true."

"They're going to get sued so bad," Janine said, hugging herself. "The FBI, the CIA, the Maronne PD, whoever the fuck." Mrs. Tela did not react to this word, and neither did the Markos. "They let Ron's wife out an hour ago and she just walked home. She was wandering around here, back and forth over the bridge. They're gonna get sued for *ev-ry-thing*. Lost wages and pain and suffering for everybody." She swung her arm out. "Pain and suffering times a hundred and fifty people."

Livy's mother followed the arc of her arm. "Where is everybody? It's so quiet."

"In jail," Mrs. Tela said. "Or staying inside."

※

First, Livy slept. She slept for seventeen hours. The next morning her alarm shrieked and she jerked awake, sweaty, panicking, her lungs not drawing right, and shut it off. It was her work alarm. The electricity was back on. She lay in her too-small bed, trying to catch her breath. Did she have a job now? She could not think. They would find out about the pharmacy soon and come for her, she was sure.

She woke again hours later, the day already peaked and receding. Her mother was standing in the doorway.

"You don't leave the house until we say you can," she said. "Do you understand?"

"Yes," Livy said. Her mouth was dry. She wanted to ask her mother for water but she saw that she should not.

※

The phone rang all day. Livy's mother called her own mother and in-laws and boss, explained what had happened, asserted over and over that they were fine, and then unplugged the phone.

Livy lay in bed and wondered if Nelson was still in jail, if he was all right, if they were questioning him or charging him. She felt sure he would say nothing that wasn't true, no matter how hard they pushed, but she didn't know if that would be enough. Later, when the house felt empty, she crept downstairs and turned on the TV. The news anchor said: "A search for a wanted person goes tragically wrong. Anger in this small town over the death of a local man." Livy watched with the volume turned down low, sitting on the floor an arm's length from the screen, fighting back the vertigo of seeing it on television. All these people watching, all of a sudden—newscasters and police and an old woman from Maronne who was stopped on the sidewalk outside the SuperFresh and asked for her opinion.

Livy felt like a ghost in the old house, drifting, disordering objects quietly in the kitchen. She kept returning to the TV. There were news vans right there, in Lomath; reporters from the Philadelphia stations stood in front of the Church of God in Christ, in front of the range building in the Sportsmen's Club complex, in front of the store. Livy saw the same slow panning shot of the intersection four times, the dense green of the hill, the dust and broken-glass glitter of the road. Jocelyn was not at work, the OPEN flag was down. The intersection was empty. There were a few front-porch interviews, all among the neighbors on the other side of the bridge, pallid people Livy didn't know well. A reporter Livy remembered from several natural disasters called the place a "ghost town." The camera followed Paula Carden getting out of her blue Taurus, turning her body away from the cameras, walking deliberately up her own front steps like she was deaf.

Around five the natural disaster woman said, "A possible kidnapping," and Livy knew the police were coming back for her. Her mind was like a brick. Less than an hour later she heard them coming up the walk, and she got up off the living room floor and slipped her feet into her shoes and waited. Her mother came up the stairs.

"They're back?" she said.

"I'm sorry," Livy said. Knuckles sounded on the tin frame of the screen door.

※

This was the beginning of the worst time, when everything receded from Livy. The police kept her up all night in an interrogation room, telling her lies and making her go through the story of the pharmacy again and again, until she was confusing her own name with Nelson's and Mark's. No one mentioned Revaz. On the second day a young attorney named Beth arrived from Legal Aid, and the interrogations stopped. Livy's parents had sent her. On the third day there was a hearing and charges were announced. They were what Beth had told Livy to expect: one count of conspiracy to commit armed robbery, one count of conspiracy kidnapping, one count of accessory kidnapping after the fact, and one count of evading a roadblock. Livy had to sign papers with cuffed hands and stand with the arresting officer while Beth talked to the district attorney and conferred briefly with the judge. It was over in less than ten minutes. Livy was taken back to the police station, where her clothes were returned to her and she was released into the custody of her parents.

"Livy?" they said. "Why didn't you tell anybody about that boy?"

For a day or so Livy didn't talk; she could explain nothing, she understood nothing. She watched television and slept, and her parents circled around her, wide-eyed and anxious, occasionally angry; sometimes prodding at her silence, sometimes letting it be. She came downstairs when her parents had finished their meals and heated up the leftovers for herself in a pan. If her father found her doing this he would stand by the counter and wait for her to turn and look at him, but she wouldn't. After a while he would say, "Fine."

There had been a funeral for Ron Cash while Livy was in jail. There had been police in unmarked cars parked across the street from the funeral home, as if a riot might break out. All the folding chairs were filled and a line of overheated people in black had stretched out into the vestibule and down the front steps.

Livy would have a court date in September. At best, she would know in six weeks if she was going to jail, or to a juvenile detention center, or if she would be spared both. In the meantime she wasn't allowed to leave the house or use the phone, and she didn't try.

She was allowed to watch TV, however. The day after she came home from jail she turned on one of the twenty-four-hour news networks and found Revaz staring at her. It was the photo the police had shown people in Lomath, the rumpled gray-haired man with his look of having slept on a bus. The channel had a staccato rhythm, the photo appearing after the break every forty-five minutes with a recap, so that detail accumulated in distinct sedimentary layers. At noon his Georgian nationality was confirmed; at two thirty the Georgian consulate held a press conference and emphasized that his parents had been immigrants from Chechnya. For a while a hurricane grew peacefully at sea, and the anchors' minds were elsewhere. At five a Russian diplomat was shown speaking at some sort of dinner, the podium badly centered in the frame, the audio too low.

By six a statement had come out from the Georgians, and opposite Revaz's photo there was grainy footage of a smoking, sinking ferry in a gray river. The video had been distributed to the networks along with an official statement of the charges against him: material support in a bombing plot five years before that had killed nine people. He had fled the country just before his arraignment, which had been scheduled for the previous week. A harried Georgian diplomat described him as a mercenary for separatist-nationalist Chechen causes, a tabloid journalist who met the wrong kind of people in his line of work and was too stupid or broke to resist their offers, the kind of man who would kill nine people for a few thousand dollars. An American diplomat alluded to the possibility that the criminal network he was involved in had ties to larger groups, transnational groups, groups that were responsible for American deaths.

The ferry crossed a river in Russia. In the clip it listed on its side, attended by rescue boats, all of them dwarfed by a vast column of smoke. There was a digital animation also, with tiny peg-like human figures moving at a restrained pace away from a column of orange fire that reached up from the car hold through the middle deck of the ferry. It was terrible to watch the white lines of the deck tilt and sink. Three of the nine people who died were children.

"What is wrong with people over there?" Livy's father said. He had come in as he did every day for the evening news and was drinking his after-work beer on the sofa.

Livy said nothing. The pictures of the burning ferry took her breath away, and she had to look down at her hands as the footage played. She had a maximum-gravity feeling in the pit of her stomach, as if she were draining out through her own bowels. They were showing school portraits of the dead children. She wondered if her father would think it was strange if she stood up now and left the room.

"I hope they got what they wanted out of this," her father said, though Livy couldn't tell whether he meant the police or the people who had put the bomb on the ferry. "I hope they think it was worth it."

There was security camera footage of Revaz, or someone who looked like him, shuffling through an airport line in Poland en route to the United States. A security envoy held a press conference confirming the charges, alluding only indirectly to roadblocks and the death of Ron Cash. Video of Shelly Cash outside the police station was shown again, her face all pulled out of shape from crying.

Livy was horrified, but had to appear to be interested only in the normal way, and she wasn't sure what that was. As the news coverage rolled on and on she tried to take her cues from her father: blunted anger when the siege was discussed, an undertow of what-do-you-expect; at each sight of the burning ferry, a brief silence. There was a clip of the director of some national security suboffice mumbling into a microphone, bland and uninformative, pausing at one point to sweep a little wave of gray hair back off of his forehead. He said several times that information on the case was limited by an ongoing investigation, by the fact that other suspects were still at large in Chechnya and Russia, by security concerns.

After her parents had gone to bed she returned to the television. Russian diplomats gave interviews, some of them smooth and quiet, some thundering. They called Revaz a sociopath, a mobster, a drunk with unpayable debts. And then Revaz's sister appeared, a middle-aged woman with short blonde hair, a neat hard face, wide eyes.

Livy was grateful that she was alone when the sister appeared, because the resemblance to Revaz was so striking that she jumped. The woman was exasperated and looked like she hadn't slept in days. She was interviewed via satellite from her home in Paris, where she sat wearing a dark suit, leaning closer to the camera as the pitch of her voice rose. *Anna Deni Fournier* said the screen. "My brother has never been to Chechnya," she said. "We are Georgians with a Chechen name. Our parents were from Chechnya. They are dead. We are Georgians."

It made Livy sweat to watch her. "This is corruption, you do not understand our politics, he is a journalist," Anna said. "He was writing stories about corruption. They want him to be quiet so they make accusations. They want him to be dead so he will stop bothering."

Livy imagined the nervous speechless man in the garage first as a murdering terrorist (craven, subtly manipulating her with his shows of helplessness, laughing at her when he was alone) and then as a persecuted journalist (panicked, grateful, his bewildered looks sincere, his caution hiding a deep gentleness). It was like switching out a white lightbulb for a red one and watching the room change.

She turned the TV off and wandered around the house, upstairs and down. She had a sudden keen desire to get high. She was frenzied and electrified by this contact with the world—the much, much wider world—but she could tell no one. She couldn't even speak to Nelson about it, because her only avenue of contact with him was the internet, which she knew was not safe. It made her feel dizzyingly alone. She rolled a joint from the stash in the music box and lay still. Once in a great while a car would pass on Prospect

Road and white headlights would sweep across the
ceiling of her room.

※

Revaz slept under a picnic table for two nights outside
Pittsburgh, waiting for Davit's cousin, making visits to
a rest stop food court across the road twice a day to pick
up leftovers abandoned on the tables. It was mostly fried
chicken, great expanses of hard, brown material that suggested birds the size of cattle. He had to pause each time
at the door before he went in, willing himself into a state
of calm, knowing that only confidence could make him
invisible. He was beginning to take a little pride in his
ability to keep body and soul together. Wasn't that some
kind of virtue? He liked to think it showed the same
wholesome energy as any other living thing, a mouse, a
fish. His clothes were filthy. His money was gone.

The cousin's blue tractor-trailer eased into the rest
stop parking lot at eleven thirty on the morning of the
third day, massive and gleaming, with airbrushed lightning bolts along the sides of the cab. Revaz watched
from across the parking lot as the cousin stepped down
from the cab and lit a cigarette. He was wearing ridiculous wraparound sunglasses. Tbilisi emanated from him
like a smell. Revaz approached quickly, his head down.

"Revaz?" the cousin said.

"Yes."

"Koba." He offered his hand. "You look like shit."

Revaz felt a rush of emotion at the sound of his own language. Yes, he looked like shit. It sounded exactly right. "You have an extra cigarette?" he said.

"No such thing," Koba said, but he handed him one.

In the cab, Koba listened to a radio show that he informed Revaz was about sports, and broke into angry exclamations in English about basketball. He was twenty-four years old and had lived in the United States since he was nineteen. He loved basketball. He was driving the truck to Arizona. He might get another load there and go on to California. "You should hope we go to California," he said to Revaz, with something like a leer, not feeling the need to elaborate. An enameled cross and a foam-rubber basketball hung over the dashboard. He settled into a stream of commentary about the gray landscape, the occasional views of deep valleys, the broad rivers opening up and closing again one after another.

"The plane crashed near here," Koba said at one point, and Revaz didn't know what plane he meant, but didn't ask. It occurred to him that Koba was lonely too, driving the truck for weeks at a time by himself. Revaz kept quiet and let the chatter wash over him. He was falling asleep, the broad stuffed seat like a lap to lie in, the road humming beneath, the voice going on and on.

✻

One night Livy woke at two and knew she wouldn't go back to sleep. Her mind was going back and forth on its single anxious track, *zzt-zzt, zzt-zzt,* like the ink carriage in an old printer. It was only five weeks until her court date. Lately she had been thinking about the surveillance video from the pharmacy: What did it look like? An image like an ultrasound, four stuttering figures in light and dark, Dominic's upraised arm with the gun, and herself: walking around the counter and standing beside Mark. She was the closest to him, the one at his elbow while he counted out the pills, her own arms folded. Could her face be read? Where was Nelson in the frame? After she had gone behind the counter she had lost track of the rest of them, somehow. The world had gotten very small. Did she look cruel, those crossed arms, the invasion of the space behind the counter while the boys stood apart? Mark was all right. The police had gathered him up after the tear-gassing, picked apart his story, sent him home. On television they said it was an ordeal for his family, and she thought about his family often now. A sister and a mother, baffled and afraid.

Sometimes she felt sure she was going to jail, and often she thought she deserved it.

Around the side of the house she could see the surfaceless dark of the clump of trees where she had seen her parents burning their crop. There had been no mention of it since she came home; they didn't seem to know she knew about it. She wanted to see the campfire up close. She crossed the yard and picked her way into the wash. She found the remains of the fire and rubbed the ash between her fingers: that sharp smell.

The water was loud and she didn't hear her mother coming at all. She saw the beam of the flashlight first, searching across the trees.

"Livy!" her mother called.

She crouched, shrank against a rock.

"Livy, come on," her mother said. The flashlight switched off and she stood at the edge of the yard, motionless, looking over toward the driveway. Livy cursed under her breath. She couldn't watch her mother look in the wrong direction, straining to hear. She stood up. "I'm here," she called.

The flashlight clicked back on. Livy shaded her eyes. "I'm coming out." She pushed her way back out into the yard.

"I checked on you and you were gone," her mother said.

"You check on me?"

"Sometimes. Why were you there?" She pointed at the wash.

Livy wanted the two of them to be having a moment of understanding. She wanted to be able to reassure her mother, say: *I know you did something stupid but it's all right now.* They could trade indulgences, one fuckup for another. The plants for everything Livy had done. But there was no real comparison and it was too dark to read her mother's face anyway.

"No reason," Livy said.

✳

"Can I call Nelson?" Livy said. Her mother was unloading the washing machine and Livy was hovering in the doorway, half watching the television in the next room. Livy's mother looked up from the laundry basket. "You want to use the phone?"

"Please."

Livy's mother held up a pair of Livy's jeans and shook them out. "Did I ever tell you I stole my mother's car once?"

"What? You did?"

"I was fifteen. I had these older friends I was trying to impress. So I took the keys out of her purse and took the car."

"What'd she do?"

"She called the police. She knew it was me, but she called the police."

Livy's grandmother was a haughty, ancient woman who flew in twice a year and distributed birthday checks. Livy's mother became slightly unhinged around her, setting out cloth napkins, harassing her family into more polite versions of themselves.

"Did they arrest you?" Livy said.

"Yes, they did. I spent two days in jail while she thought about whether she wanted to press charges. We were already having a tough time there, getting-along-wise." She shut the lid of the washing machine. "My grandma talked her out of it. So she let me come home."

Livy searched for the relevance of the anecdote. "Did she punish you?"

Livy's mother sighed. "She knocked my head against a wall, and then she felt so bad about it she never mentioned it again."

Livy blinked. She was getting to an age when family information was shared with her that had been hidden when she was little. People were always so casual when they told stories like this; their voices gave you no hints about how to react. "Were you mad?"

"Oh, I don't know. I was fifteen." Livy's mother looked at her. "I guess I'm trying to make myself look good by comparison."

"You're way nicer than she is."

Her mother laughed. She was quiet for a minute. "I can't tell if I'm punishing you too much or not enough," she said. "Go ahead and call him, though. You must be lonely."

Livy took the cordless out to the porch and dialed the number. Mrs. Tela picked up.

"Is Nelson there?" Livy said.

There was a pause, and then Mrs. Tela sighed. "Is this Livy?" she said.

"Yes."

"You can't talk to him, Livy."

Livy felt a little hiccup, an interruption in the atmosphere. "He's not there?"

"I'm not letting you talk to him." Mrs. Tela sounded tired and reasonable, like someone correcting an error in her gas bill. "You went to jail together, Livy. I don't think you can be friends anymore."

Livy stared at the trunk of the ash tree by the porch. "Until when?"

"I'm surprised your parents are even letting you call. Bye now, Livy." The line beeped and went dead. Livy paced for a minute at the edge of the porch, running her thumb back and forth over the hot part of the phone where it had been pressed against her cheek. Then she sat down on the floorboards and started to cry. It was a little trickle of tears, no sobbing, very quiet.

The cicadas were making their cascading call all across the yard. It would start to get cool soon. School would start. She would sit in the yellow light of her room over a trigonometry book and listen to the same four albums over and over and hear the dishes being washed in the kitchen, know it was all ruined, and have no one to talk to. Then, at the end of September, her court date.

The long open days were almost gone and they would never be allowed to be friends as they had been friends. And she loved him, maybe. She used the words surreptitiously and self-mockingly, even in her own mind. She seemed to love him. It appeared that she loved him. She tried it out, tasted it, stared out into the yard.

✼

When Livy stepped onto the bus on the first day of school she met a wall of eyes. She glanced sideways at the driver, expecting the bored profile she'd seen twice a day for two years, the elaborate and refreshing lack of interest; but the bus driver was also staring at her. Livy picked her way down the aisle in total silence. The narrow space required a complicated set of movements she had never noticed before, a baffling series of choices— look up or down? Drop the bag on the seat first, or sit down and drag it in after? Fold hands? She clutched the bag and studied the window, the dirt on the glass, until the bus was moving again.

A week before, the vice principal had called, suggesting to Livy's mother that Livy might consider short-term homeschooling until her case was resolved. Her mother had said that whatever happened with Livy had not occurred on school grounds and was therefore irrelevant to the vice principal's interests, and to the school board, and to anyone else who might be concerned. And that was that.

Lomath was gone in a moment. There were no other pickups; Dominic always got a ride with someone, and Nelson's mother dropped him off when she took his sister to her private school. Lomath looked quiet, the hills just touched with light. It seemed clear to her already that the day would be just as bad as she'd thought.

Maronne Consolidated was a large, low brick building moated with parking lots. In the front stairwell she passed a boy who had once washed dishes at the Lomath Sportsmen's Club. He'd gotten fired in July and made an impressive scene about it, despite being stoned. He even pulled his apron off and hurled it into the sink at the appropriate moment.

"Hey, the restaurant's closed now, isn't it?" he said.

She stopped. "Yeah, it's closed." The owner had not come to reopen it and she didn't know if he ever would.

The business had been on the edge of failure even before the blockade, and every mention of it on the news was more bad press, reporters talking about the guns in the pro shop as if it were a militia stockpile and not a large beige building with a sports and recreation license.

"Is it because of the cops shooting that guy?" he said.

She stared at him.

"Did they fuck you up?" he said. He was bright with interest, excited, but he put a casual drawl on the words "fuck you up" as if this were a situation he encountered often himself, getting fucked up by the police. She grasped now that he was edging around the main question, leaning closer and closer, his backpack nearly toppling him. He lowered his voice. "Did you seriously kidnap that guy?" he said.

She stepped back with a startled expression, like an ingenue in a silent movie. "Fuck you," she said. She did her best to disappear in the crowd at the bottom of the stairs.

In her homeroom the staring was gradual. She was one of the first to arrive, so it took a while for the normal buzz of conversation to build up in the room, and then a few minutes more for her presence to be noted and commented on. Livy had brought a book to read, a ridiculous ploy, since it was not normal to read books in homeroom on the first day of school; it only made her more obvious, the single bowed head in the room. She read the same sentence over and over again while seats shifted around her, chair legs scraped, and people whispered.

She had hoped she might have the same lunch period as Nelson. At twelve thirty she stood at the door to the cafeteria with her lunch tray, scanning the room, but he wasn't there. Her chest constricted. Disappointment was hard to bear when she wanted such small things: half an hour with him. To talk to him, which would relieve her of the work of imagining what it was like to talk to him, evaluating the strength of her feelings that way, biting them like coins.

A girl named Valeria who'd been in a play with Livy the year before waved at her, and Livy sat down quickly at her table. Valeria talked and talked, and appeared not to notice when people at neighboring tables twisted on their benches to look at Livy. Livy was at a loss to explain this generosity, but she accepted it quietly. Valeria had spent the summer working at a store in the mall that sold leather jackets and she had stories to tell about many of their classmates who worked in other stores. From the sound of it, they had formed a little kingdom rich in intrigue there among the fountains and the potted ferns. There were betrayals and drugs and secret abortions. Managers pursued young girls. Scores were settled outside, or deferred to other parking lots where there was less security. Livy listened for thirty minutes and then they were dismissed.

In the hallway she saw Elena, she of the Honor Society and the ritualistic diner trips. She was putting her books away. She stood and turned, saw Livy, and went white in the face.

"Why are you looking at me like that?" Livy said.

"Somebody told me you were here but I thought they were lying," Elena said. "I thought you must be in jail or something."

Pain bubbled up in Livy. "I haven't even had my court date yet. You could have called and found out."

"My mom won't let me talk to you. She said she would take my car keys if she found out I did."

"Nelson's mom won't let me talk to him either," Livy said.

"Oh, she's keeping him home from school," Elena said. "She's trying to get him into Sacred Heart with his sister."

"He's not coming to school?" Another beam gave way inside her.

"Of course not. I mean, you guys—" Elena sighed, peered more closely at Livy's face. "You guys did something *really serious*. I didn't even know you hung out with Dominic." She shook her head. "I have to go to class."

"Go," Livy said. "Say hello to your mom for me."

She watched Elena disappear around the corner. Crowds milled and circulated. *All the extra stuff falls away*, she thought. *Pretty soon it'll be just me, sitting on a rock.*

※

In the end, there was a plea. Livy's lawyer met with the district attorney at the end of September and the deal came back two days later. "They're hanging on to the accessory charge," her lawyer said on the phone, apologetic, mumbling a bit so Livy had to press the handset to her ear. "Your record's good and the whole situation is embarrassing so they didn't push for juvenile detention. They're offering six months' house arrest and probation until you're eighteen." She cleared her throat. "If you stay out of trouble your record will be sealed."

"Six months' house arrest?" Livy was standing at the kitchen window with the cordless phone, twisting a rubber band around her wrist. "I'm not going to jail?"

"Not if you take this."

"I'm taking it."

"I have to talk to your parents."

"I'll tell them to call you. They're at work."

After she hung up the phone she walked outside barefoot, warmed by relief. It was late September and the ground was cold already. The Inskys' farm was touched with absurd gold, held up there at the end of the valley;

she stood in the yard looking at it, and then walked down
to the creek and sat with her arms around her knees. It
would all be all right. House arrest would be humiliating and isolating but she could get through six months.
A year after that she would be eighteen and it would be
as if this never happened. In some ways it already felt
like Revaz had never happened. He was a ghost, a story
that only Nelson knew. He would be her currency of
intimacy. Many people might know little things about
her but there would be very few in her whole life, she
thought, who would hear this secret. It would always be
with her, right there at her elbow. That was what made
you grown-up, she thought: having the past following
you around. Having a past at all, really.

※

The fog was astonishing, a solid object heaped up over
the city's shoulders, rolling down with an illusion of
slowness created by its immensity, little winds pulling
threads from its surface as if it were made of cotton
wool. Every afternoon it loomed histrionically over the
parks of San Francisco and Revaz stared at it, and no
one else seemed to notice it at all. Long ago, when he'd
visited the mountains in the summers in Georgia, there
had been morning mist over the trees; but it was still and

transparent, burning off at the first full light. This was an oceanic phenomenon. He sometimes bought an ice cream cone at a cart just off Dolores Park and watched it come in. The teenagers lounging on the grass shrugged into windbreakers as it descended.

Koba gave Revaz some advice before dropping him off in Oakland. "Get some Mexican friends," he said. "They know where the work is. And tell people you're Russian. They won't know the difference."

"Russians will know the difference," Revaz said.

"That's true," Koba said. He rubbed his chin for a minute, as if this were a weighty intellectual puzzle. "Okay, you tell the Russians you're Georgian. With them you can be honest, because you know they don't give a shit. But never"—here he turned and grinned, giving Revaz's arm a firm squeeze—"tell them you're Chechen."

"I'm not Chechen, you asshole."

"You are. You're a Chechen Georgian asshole. And here I leave you."

He gestured out at the road. Revaz nodded, looking through the windshield, gathering himself for a minute. Then he said, "Thank you," and climbed down, heaving the door shut behind him. Koba lit a cigarette and waved. That was the last time they saw each other.

Revaz slept in a gravel lot under a piece of plastic sheeting that night, and in the morning walked four miles to a parking lot off the Berkeley Marina where day laborers gathered. No one seemed remotely curious about his nationality. He had picked up a few English words but was beginning to learn that for most business, gestures and circumstances did the work. He did not have to achieve invisibility here; it was freely conferred on him. For a few days in a row he was picked up by a passenger van and taken to a supermarket in Lake Merritt to unload trucks. He worked ostentatiously hard, loading his dolly higher than others at the expense of his back. He even found a plastic broom with a bent handle in a corner of the loading dock, and when they were finished unloading he would sweep up the scraps of wilting lettuce and corn silk and crushed flowers. In the second week, the driver of the van indicated that he could come directly to the store in the mornings, which Revaz took to mean that he had a job.

There were orange flowers everywhere, heaps of vines in the small, square front yards of the bungalows along Piedmont Avenue. Koba had not prepared him for the peculiar dry lushness of the East Bay, the purple blooms winding around massive cactuses, the persimmon trees glowing in the shadows behind fences. It was September, but the place completely lacked the urgency he had always felt in the autumn in Georgia, the sense that light and warmth were draining away and would soon be gone. The warmth lingered. There was no great change afoot as the days turned toward October.

He chose a fake name. He kept his ID duct-taped to the back of a ceiling tile in his room, a place he paid for by the week, accepting reduced rent in exchange for clearing dead weeds out of the yard and hauling out the trash on Tuesdays and Fridays. His landlady was Georgian, the only one he had encountered so far in California. It would have been smarter to avoid her for this reason, he supposed; and it would have been smarter to destroy the ID. But it was not so easy to do these things. Sometimes he took the easy way and hoped for luck. Most of the time, really, if he was being very honest with himself.

Had he paid yet? The thought woke him sometimes at night. Sometimes, if he'd been drinking before going to bed, he made earnest attempts to answer the question. He had known the wrong people, certainly, and he had not asked many questions. There was a row of figures to line up, the left and the right. But when he was sober, he recognized the superstitious nature of these mathematics. There could be no settling up.

Once, while Revaz was unpacking crates of tomatillos in a stockroom at five thirty in the morning, the PA system unexpectedly switched on in the main body of the store. There was a startling crackle and then Otis

Redding, already well into the chorus, sang out "Sittin' On The Dock of the Bay" over the empty aisles, the PA turned up so high that it echoed out to the parking lot. Revaz was suddenly flushed, the hair standing up on the back of his neck. He went to the loading doors to cool down. An old girlfriend—years and years ago, when he was not yet thirty—had given him a cassette with that song and a few others on it and explained the thrust of the lyrics, teasing him for his ignorance of English. It was his favorite from the cassette. He could see her apartment; he could smell it, the mold and the fresh paint she was trying to cover it with, the floor cleaner she used, the tea boiling on the stove. There were tears in his eyes. One of the other men unloading the truck was singing along in a full-throated baritone, and he stopped in front of the lump of Revaz at the edge of the loading dock and shouted happily in his face, "California! California!" and Revaz nodded and smiled, because he supposed that did have something to do with it—brushing the tears away with fingers that smelled like oranges—it was his old girlfriend who was gone forever now but it was also California, it was coming to the place in the song even though he had not meant to, crossing over.

✳

In October, Nelson was back in school. Livy had been expecting this since she got her plea. They'd given him the same deal. Dominic and Brian, because they had brought the gun, got worse: they would each spend nearly a year in juvenile detention. Livy had heard that Nelson couldn't get into Sacred Heart this year and his mother was sending him back to Maronne Consolidated. The news unsettled her for two days before she saw him.

She spotted him through the open gymnasium door as she was walking back to her locker after lunch. She stopped immediately. He was standing by the far wall, waiting for his turn to kick a ball. He was paying attention to the game; his head moved when the ball sailed up. There was something strangely suspended about sound in big wooden spaces like the gym, Livy thought. The shouts and collisions took forever to settle, to end.

She wanted to talk to him, but he looked fine, ordinary and at peace in a clump of other boys, and she wondered if he wasn't better off away from her, like his mother said. Hadn't they caused a lot of trouble for each other? He reached up and rubbed his nose with the back of his hand and for a second she saw what she was— a visitor, observing and unobserved, about to break the peace.

She often thought now about the power everybody had to ruin everybody else. You could do it by accident, just by showing up, or you could make the wrong decisions in such small pieces that by the time you realized what you were doing, it was too late. Knowing this should have made her timid and anxious but instead she could feel it making her big, because she knew now that the worst thing could happen and you would find yourself still alive afterward, your eyes still open. In a year and a half she would be eighteen and free, headed someplace new.

Nelson turned and saw her and she waved at him. He glanced over at the teacher and assistant coach: they were absorbed in conversation by the locker room doors. He left his place in line and walked over to her, rubbing the back of his neck, trying to look casual.

"You're back," she said. She closed her fingers briefly around his wrist and then let go, too jittery to hold on. How bizarre that they hadn't seen each other since they were both lying in the road that day.

"It's nice to see you," he said.

Her mouth was dry; she thought of touching his wrist again but only splayed her fingers briefly in the air at her side. "Do you think you can get out of here for a minute? So we can talk?" she said.

He looked back over his shoulder at the teacher again, and then stepped around the door and into the hallway. "Yeah, let's go," he said.

They walked quickly. Her heartbeat sped up; someone might come around a corner at any moment and
ask to see a pass. The doors at the end of the hall were
propped open and sweet air flowed in. They stepped
outside, onto the grass. The parking lots were quiet; the
building hummed.

"Where do we go?" Livy said.

Nelson scanned the quiet scene, the road where security guards cruising in Jeeps might appear at any moment, the distant highway lifted on an embankment.
"There," he said, pointing into the trees.

The woods began behind the stadium. Livy and Nelson skirted the massive aluminum structure as fast as
they could, hand in hand. It was mid-October but the
trees were still in full leaf and the day was warm and
bright; it was lovely and faintly wrong, as if they were
receiving some beneficence that had been left there by
accident. Once they were inside the margin of the trees
Livy was overwhelmed by the most basic kind of relief:
being out of sight at last.

"You think security comes in here?" she said. She
grinned and hugged him.

"I missed you," he said. He squeezed her. She had
wondered if they would behave like friends when they
saw each other again, but she was alight with adrenaline from escaping the school building and the decision

seemed to be making itself, yanking her along with it. She kissed him on the mouth too hard, felt his teeth, put her arms around him. She sat down abruptly on the ground and pulled him with her.

He pushed her skirt up a little. He was shy. She pressed her legs against him. She didn't often wear a skirt and she didn't know how to manage it, how to smooth it beneath her; it had bunched up in the back when she sat down, and she could feel the damp earth through her underwear. Their eyes tracked each other, too close to focus.

"I don't know when I'll see you again," she said, and now she felt the heat of tears under her eyelids. She would be fitted soon with an ankle monitor and so would he. They would not be allowed to see each other for some time. There would be a long solitude. At the end of it they might be different people entirely. There was nothing to say about this, no way to reach forward into the unknowable future and make promises about what would happen there. Livy felt equal and opposite impulses—first to bolt, to flee the exposure she felt, and second to burrow into him.

"I'll send you letters," he said. "From up the hill."

They had left their bags behind and they would be in trouble when they got home—the attendance secretary would have called. But they weren't in trouble yet. No one knew where they were. They hardly existed here; it was quiet, and though the shade was deep beneath the trees, the air was warm.

ACKNOWLEDGEMENTS

Thanks to Soumeya Roberts at Writers House for taking a chance on me, for sticking it out through round after round, and for ordering pink champagne in French. Thanks to Masie Cochran at Tin House for making my dream come true, which is the only way to say it. Thanks to Nanci McCloskey and Meg Cassidy for your energy and creativity. Thanks to Diane Chonette for a perfect cover.

Thank you to Peter and Katie Knecht, who know that if there's a will, there's a way. Thanks to Rastus Knecht for being, as ever, cooler than me.

Thanks to my most rigorous, kind, and inventive readers, who are also brilliant writers: Bonnie Altucher, Tom Cook, Jenna Leigh Evans, Roberta Newman, and Helen Terndrup. Thanks to Hannah Elnan, who did me many favors and gave me many dry goods and preserves.

Thanks to the Center for Fiction, for your generosity and support. Thanks to New Directions, Barbara Epler, and Laurie Callahan, for rewarding my bad manners. Thanks to Dan Chaon, who took me seriously when there was no reason to do so, and to Sharon Law, a beautiful teacher who is deeply missed.

Thanks to Pauline Jennings, who was larger than life, and Ted Fairbanks, who held court for twenty years.

Thanks in advance to my large and tolerant family for not reading anything too literally.

Thanks to Mark, for coming along.

BOOK CLUB QUESTIONS

1. Whom do you think of as the antagonist in this novel? Is it Dominic? Revaz? The townspeople? The police? Or someone/thing else entirely?

2. What sort of ending do you imagine for Revaz?

3. What were you expecting from Livy and Nelson's relationship? How do you think Knecht balances the intense friendship and the budding romance?

4. How do you think the relationship between Livy and her parents evolves throughout the book?

5. The cover design features illustrations of thistles that are both beautiful and dangerous. How is this idea reflected in the town's isolation and remote location?

6. Which story of a citizen of Lomath would you like to know more about? Why?